THE MYSTERY OF THE FINAL LAP

A LADY MILDRED RAMSAY MURDER MYSTERY

RUTH BAKER

CLEANTALES PUBLISHING

Copyright © CleanTales Publishing

First published in October 2025

All characters and events in this publication, other than those clearly in the public domain, are fictitious and any resemblance to real persons, living or dead, is purely coincidental.

Copyright © CleanTales Publishing

The moral right of the author has been asserted.

All rights reserved. This book or any portion thereof may not be reproduced or used in any manner whatsoever without the express written permission of the publisher except for the use of brief quotations in a book review.

For questions and comments about this book, please contact info@cleantales.com

ISBN: 9798267943406
Imprint: Independently Published

OTHER BOOKS IN THE LADY MILDRED RAMSAY MURDER MYSTERY SERIES

The Mystery of the Disappearing Diamonds

The Mystery of the Final Lap

The Mystery of the Vanishing Violinist

A LADY MILDRED RAMSAY MURDER MYSTERY

BOOK TWO

1

Lady Mildred Ramsay considered herself a woman of moderate temperament, neither overly excitable nor particularly placid. But as the motorcar rounded the final bend in the Surrey lane and the Brooklands circuit came into view, she felt a most immoderate flutter of anticipation in her chest.

"Oh, Mildred, look at that!" Lady Beatrice Mortimer—Bea to all who knew her longer than a quarter-hour—leaned so far forward in her seat that the chauffeur shot a concerned glance in the rear-view mirror. "It's enormous! Like a great Roman colosseum, but for motorcars instead of gladiators."

Mildred adjusted her cloche hat, which the morning breeze had tugged slightly askew. "I believe the comparison was intentional when they built it. Though I daresay the Romans had fewer advertisements for motor oil."

Before them, the concrete banking of the Brooklands Motor Circuit rose like a great grey wave frozen in time, its steep outer walls emblazoned with painted signs proclaiming the virtues of Castrol, Shell, and Dunlop. Even at half-past nine in the morning, the air vibrated with the growl of engines being tuned, tested, and coaxed into higher states of readiness.

"I've never understood why men insist on making engines so thunderously loud," Mildred remarked, as Watkins, her brother's chauffeur, slowed the Daimler to navigate the gravel approach. "One would think a well-engineered machine might whisper rather than roar."

"But then how would everyone know you're terribly important and have an expensive motorcar?" Bea countered with a grin.

Watkins guided the Daimler to a halt alongside a row of similarly handsome vehicles, their gleaming bonnets catching the late autumn sunshine.

"Thank you, Watkins," Mildred said as he opened her door. "I believe we'll be quite some time. The charity presentations aren't scheduled until two, and I suspect Lady Beatrice will insist on witnessing every race and possibly crawling beneath several motorcars."

"I shall only crawl beneath the most fashionable ones," Bea corrected, already halfway out of the car. Her pale blue dress, chosen specifically to complement the Brooklands colours, fluttered in the same breeze that carried the scent of petrol, oil, and something sweetly spiced that suggested the Clubhouse kitchens were already busy.

Watkins offered a small bow. "Very good, my lady. I'll remain available."

As they approached the entrance, a ramrod-straight figure in an immaculate brown suit separated himself from the gatekeepers. He advanced with the precise, measured stride of a man who had spent his life ensuring that trains departed exactly on schedule.

THE MYSTERY OF THE FINAL LAP

"Lady Ramsay, Lady Mortimer. Edwin Hartley, circuit steward." He executed a small, mechanically perfect bow. "You are precisely on time."

He reached into his waistcoat and withdrew not one but two pocket watches, checking them simultaneously before returning them to their respective pockets.

"How splendid," Bea remarked. "Two watches. In case one stops?"

"In case one is incorrect, Lady Mortimer," Hartley replied without a trace of humour. "A discrepancy of even thirty seconds can be the difference between victory and defeat on the curve of the track. Your donation presentation is scheduled for 1400 hours exactly. Captain Mallory's demonstration lap will commence at thirteen forty-five, followed by the ladies' committee address at thirteen fifty-five, and your presentation at fourteen hundred."

He extended a slim folder containing what appeared to be a minute-by-minute schedule printed in a compact, precise hand.

"The Members' Enclosure is open for morning tea. The paddock inspection you requested has been arranged for ten-fifteen. Any deviation will necessitate adjustments to subsequent timings."

Mildred accepted the folder with a grave nod that matched Hartley's solemnity. "Your precision is admirable, Mr Hartley."

"Precision is safety, Lady Ramsay. Especially at Brooklands."

As he turned away to intercept another arrival, Bea whispered, "Good heavens. Do you suppose he schedules his meals by the second?"

"I imagine Mr Hartley has never been surprised by an undercooked potato in his life," Mildred replied. "Though I find his devotion to order rather reassuring. Places like this —" she gestured toward the circuit, where the engines were growing more numerous and insistent "—thrive on control. Until they don't."

They made their way through the entrance and along a neat gravel path towards the Clubhouse, a handsome red-brick structure that combined Edwardian solidity with a hint of modern sleekness in its cleaner lines and larger windows. Mildred noted how the building seemed to balance the past and future, much like Brooklands itself, straddling the fading grandeur of pre-war certainties and the headlong rush of the modern 1920s.

"I'm going to inspect the paddock first," Mildred decided, glancing at Hartley's schedule. "We have almost forty minutes before our official tour."

"Forty-two minutes and sixteen seconds, according to our friend Mr Hartley," Bea corrected. "I'll join you shortly. I simply must investigate whatever is creating that heavenly aroma from the Clubhouse."

Mildred smiled indulgently. "Reconnaissance by cake?"

"The most pleasant kind. And I'll have you know that kitchens are absolute troves of information. Cooks know everything."

With that, Bea set off toward the Clubhouse, her blue dress a bright flag among the more soberly attired club members already gathering on the terrace. Mildred took the opposite path, one that led down toward the paddock area where the racing machines were prepared.

The paddock was busy with focused activity. Mildred observed how mechanics worked with practiced efficiency, their movements revealing the hierarchy and relationships that governed this technical world. Drivers in their distinctive white overalls strode between the stalls, conferring in low voices and occasionally tapping gauges or running gloved hands along streamlined bonnets.

And on the edges, like remoras attending sharks, hovered the press—notepads at the ready, pencils tucked behind ears, cameras dangling from leather straps. They watched the mechanics and drivers with the keen-eyed patience of naturalists, waiting for the moment when routine gave way to something worth recording.

Mildred moved carefully along the periphery, absorbing the rhythm of the place. A toolkit passed from hand to hand without a word being spoken. A nod between a driver and mechanic that conveyed complete understanding. The way certain journalists were permitted closer than others, the hierarchy as clear as if they wore insignia.

She paused near a brilliant green Bentley, its bonnet up to reveal an engine whose complexity reminded her of the intricate watch mechanisms her father had once shown her. A figure in oil-stained overalls straightened up from the engine, revealing itself to be a woman—slight but wiry, with close-cropped dark hair and a face that combined classical beauty with an almost stern composure.

The woman wiped her hands on a rag and shot Mildred an appraising glance, neither hostile nor welcoming. She seemed to be waiting for Mildred to betray herself as either a nuisance or someone worth acknowledging.

"You've adjusted the fuel mixture," Mildred said, gesturing to the engine.

Something flickered in the woman's eyes; surprise, swiftly masked.

"For the banking," the woman replied after a moment. "The mixture runs leaner at speed on the incline."

Mildred nodded. "My brother had similar troubles with his Alvis on steep climbs in the Lake District. Though at considerably lower speeds, I imagine."

The woman's posture relaxed marginally. "You're Lady Ramsay."

"And you would be Miss St John. I recognised your Bentley from The Autocar."

Aurelia "Rae" St John nodded once, an economical gesture that seemed characteristic of her every movement. "You're here for the charity presentation."

"And the racing," Mildred added. "I find mechanical precision rather fascinating."

Rae's mouth curved in what might have been the beginning of a smile. "It's the imprecisions that make it interesting. Anyone can build a clock. It takes art to make a racing engine."

A young man in racing whites approached, his expression hovering between deference and urgency. "Miss St John, Captain Mallory's asking for you. Something about the demonstra—" He faltered as he noticed Mildred.

"Lady Ramsay, this is Peter Finch, my apprentice," Rae said. "Peter, Lady Mildred Ramsay."

The young man executed an awkward half-bow. "An honour, my lady."

"Mr Finch." Mildred acknowledged him with a nod. "Please don't let me delay Miss St John if Captain Mallory needs her."

Rae was already reaching for a leather jacket. "Duty calls. The demonstration runs begin at eleven. The Ladies' Enclosure has the best view of the Member's Banking."

She strode away, Finch hurrying to match her pace. Mildred watched them go, noting the way other mechanics and drivers subtly tracked Rae's movement—some with respect, others with less charitable expressions.

"She's rather good, you know."

The voice—male, educated, with the particular dry delivery that belonged to neither Oxford nor Cambridge but the particular hybrid of both that Scotland Yard seemed to cultivate, came from just behind Mildred's left shoulder.

She turned, unsurprised to find Detective Inspector Charles Kent standing there, looking as inconspicuous as a man of his height and bearing could manage. He wore a well-cut suit in charcoal grey, the plainness of which was belied by its evident quality. To the casual observer, he might have passed for a well-to-do enthusiast rather than a policeman.

"Good morning, Inspector Kent," Mildred said. "How curious to find you at a motor racing circuit. Have you developed a sudden interest in carburation?"

"Good morning, Lady Ramsay." Kent's mouth twitched in what Mildred had come to recognise as his version of a smile. "Purely coincidental, I assure you. Like yourself, I'm here as a guest."

"A guest with an official capacity, I presume."

Kent glanced around the paddock with the seemingly casual but entirely deliberate observation that was his professional hallmark. "The commissioner accepted an invitation to today's charity event. He was called away to Whitehall, and I've been delegated in his place."

"How convenient," Mildred remarked. "And here I thought we might enjoy a day without murders or mysteries."

"The day is young, Lady Ramsay. I wouldn't despair of enjoying the racing just yet."

A comfortable silence settled between them, the kind that forms between two people who have seen enough of each other's capabilities to dispense with unnecessary conversation.

Finally, Kent spoke again. "I see Lady Beatrice has accompanied you today."

Mildred followed his gaze toward the Clubhouse, where Bea was emerging onto the terrace, deep in animated conversation with a white-aproned woman who was almost certainly the cook or pastry chef. Several club members were already gravitating toward Bea, drawn by her infectious enthusiasm.

"Bea considers it her personal responsibility to ensure I don't become a recluse," Mildred said. "She believes exposure to high speeds and engine noise is the key to a well-rounded character."

"And to meeting eligible gentlemen with motorcar interests, perhaps?"

"If that were her aim, I fear she's chosen the wrong companion. I tend to reduce her success rate in that department considerably."

Kent's eyebrow arched slightly. "By frightening them away with your intellect, or by solving their murders before romance can bloom?"

"A combination of both, I suspect," Mildred replied. "Though I believe the murder investigations have been the more significant deterrent."

THE MYSTERY OF THE FINAL LAP

Bea had spotted them and was now making her way down from the Clubhouse, a small napkin-wrapped package in her hand and a triumphant expression on her face.

"Mildred! Inspector Kent! You'll never guess what Mrs Thwaite has made for the luncheon." She thrust the package forward, revealing two perfect golden-brown buns. "Currant buns with ginger! Apparently, they're Captain Mallory's favourite—she makes them whenever he's racing. And she's given me her recipe."

Mildred accepted one of the buns, noting its perfect consistency. "Your reconnaissance mission was successful, I see."

"Extremely! Mrs Thwaite knows absolutely everyone. Did you know that Mr Pym, he's that dashing agent for the cable manufacturing firm, has been positively haunting Captain Mallory all week? Trying to get him to endorse some new safety cable. And Miss St John, she's the lady driver, is absolutely furious because Mallory took the demonstration slot she was promised."

Kent's expression remained neutral, but Mildred noted how his attention sharpened.

"Anything else Mrs Thwaite shared?" he asked.

Bea took a bite of her bun, her eyes sparkling. "Oh, dozens of things. That gentleman with the camera and typewriter, Mr Brooks from The Motor, has been asking all sorts of questions about fuel mixtures and brake adjustments. Hardly the usual society column material. And there's the most terrific fuss about Lady Ivy Carrington taking over the Ladies' Committee; apparently she's invested in some motor manufacturing venture, which is all very modern and shocking."

Mildred glanced at Kent, who met her eyes with the particular look they had exchanged several times before—a mutual recognition that what appeared to be Bea's social butterfly chatter often revealed the exact pressure points and fault lines that later proved critical.

"Well," Kent said, "it appears we're in for an interesting day."

"Indeed," Mildred agreed. "Though I do hope it remains merely interesting, rather than tragic."

The rising whine of an engine being tested to its limits sliced through the morning air, climbing to a pitch that set teeth on edge before settling into a throaty, powerful growl. Man and machine in perfect synchrony—until they weren't.

Mildred felt rather than saw Kent's imperceptible shift in posture, the same alertness she herself had adopted.

"Shall we walk toward the Members' Banking?" she suggested. "I believe the practice runs will be starting soon."

"An excellent suggestion, Lady Ramsay," Kent replied, offering his arm with a formal courtesy that nonetheless acknowledged their unspoken understanding.

Engines roared. Wheels turned. And somewhere in the complex machinery of Brooklands, mechanical and human alike, Mildred sensed the first faint tremors of disorder yet to come.

2

"There he is! That's Mallory's car, the silver one with the blue stripe."

Bea's excitement was infectious as she pointed toward the sleek machine now purring onto the track. The morning had advanced into a fine autumn day, the kind that English people treasure precisely because they are so rare: clear sky, gentle breeze, and sunshine that warmed rather than merely illuminated. Even the concrete banking of Brooklands seemed to soften in the golden light.

Mildred, Kent, and Bea had secured an excellent vantage point in the Members' Enclosure, a raised platform that offered an unimpeded view of the fearsome Members' Banking, the steepest part of the circuit, where cars would tilt at angles that defied common sense if not the laws of physics.

"He's rather handsome, isn't he?" Bea remarked, raising her opera glasses to better examine the driver. "All that silver at the temples and that magnificent profile."

"Captain Mallory cuts a dashing figure," Mildred noted dryly.

Captain Rex Mallory—war hero, racing driver, and darling of the Brooklands set—stood beside his car, deep in conversation with his mechanic, a burly man with rolled-up sleeves who gestured emphatically at something beneath the bonnet. Even from a distance, Mallory's bearing was unmistakable: the straight spine and squared shoulders of a military man, tempered with the easy grace of someone accustomed to moving in society's upper circles.

"He flew Sopwiths during the war," Kent remarked, his gaze intent on the scene. "Distinguished service over the Somme. Seven confirmed victories before being shot down himself. Spent six months in a German hospital before the Armistice."

Mildred glanced at him. "You seem remarkably well-informed about Captain Mallory's background, Inspector."

"The Commissioner mentioned him," Kent replied with studied casualness. "Mallory moves in influential circles. The Prince of Wales has been known to attend his races."

Below them, Mallory had donned his leather helmet and goggles. He exchanged a few more words with his mechanic, Alf Keating, if Mildred recalled the name correctly from the programme, before sliding into the driver's seat with the fluid economy of movement that spoke of long practice.

The engine note changed, rising from a purr to a snarl as Mallory engaged the gears. The car—a modified Bentley, according to the programme, though so customised as to be almost unrecognisable from its road-going cousins—began to move, gathering pace with startling rapidity.

"This is just the warm-up lap," a gentleman in tweeds, explained to his companion nearby. "He'll make two circuits to get the temperature right, then the real demonstration begins."

Around them, conversations quieted as Mallory's car circled the track, engine note rising and falling as he navigated the Byfleet Banking, the Railway Straight, and then approached the Members' Banking before them. The car moved with an almost balletic precision, finding the cleanest line through each curve.

"He's good," Kent murmured, his tone suggesting professional assessment rather than admiration.

"Very," Mildred agreed. "Though Miss St John's approach to the Byfleet Banking yesterday was, if anything, more elegant."

Kent raised an eyebrow. "You've been studying driving techniques, Lady Ramsay?"

"One never knows when such knowledge might prove useful," she replied. "Though I confess I prefer to remain firmly on the ground rather than at those angles."

Mallory's car was approaching the Members' Banking now, gathering speed along the Finishing Straight. The engine's roar echoed off the concrete, reverberating through Mildred's chest as the silver machine flashed past below them, already beginning its ascent of the banking.

The crowd drew a collective breath. Even Bea fell silent, her opera glasses tracking Mallory's progress as the car climbed higher on the banking, defying gravity through sheer velocity. There was something mesmerising about the sight: man and machine balanced on the knife-edge between control and catastrophe, separated only by skill and perhaps the thinnest margin of luck.

"Goodness, he's practically horizontal," Bea whispered.

Indeed, from their vantage point, it appeared as though Mallory and his car were attached to the banking by some invisible force, the tyres finding purchase on the concrete at an angle that made Mildred's stomach tighten involuntarily.

With one lap completed, Mallory began his second warm-up circuit. The car seemed to be moving more confidently now, the engine note steadier, the line through the curves more assured. As he rounded the Byfleet Banking once more and accelerated down the Railway Straight, a murmur of appreciation rippled through the spectators.

"He'll take the Members' Banking at full throttle this time," the tweedy gentleman informed his companion. "It's what everyone's waiting for."

The silver car approached, travelling so rapidly now that it seemed to compress the air before it. Mallory guided it onto the lower slope of the banking and began his ascent, the engine's pitch rising to a scream that set teeth on edge.

And then—a sound like a gunshot. Sharp. Definitive.

The silver car lurched suddenly, its perfect line disrupted. For one suspended moment, it seemed as though Mallory might correct the swerve through sheer will and skill. The car fishtailed, tyres fighting for purchase on the unforgiving concrete.

"Oh God," Bea breathed.

The car's right rear wheel caught the rail at the top of the banking. What happened next seemed to unfold both with the inexorable slowness of a nightmare and with the sudden brutality of reality. The Bentley cartwheeled, metal screaming against concrete, fragments spinning off in deadly trajectories. It tumbled down the banking like a child's discarded toy, finally coming to rest, crumpled and smoking, on the infield grass.

For one heartbeat, silence gripped the circuit.

Then chaos erupted. Officials sprinted toward the wreckage. Spectators surged forward, some to help, others simply drawn by the terrible magnetism of disaster. Voices rose in a cacophony of shouting, crying, and the barked commands of those trying to establish order.

Kent was already moving, taking the steps down from the Members' Enclosure two at a time. Mildred followed, her nurse's training asserting itself over shock. Bea, pale but composed, stayed close behind.

"Make way! Doctor coming through!"

The command, delivered in a crisp, authoritative female voice, cut through the tumult. The crowd parted to reveal a compact woman in her thirties, her dark hair escaping from a once-neat chignon, a medical bag clutched in one hand. She wore a tweed skirt and jacket that had seen better days, but her bearing conveyed absolute confidence.

"Dr Marsh!" someone called. "Over here!"

The doctor reached the wreckage moments before Mildred, Kent, and Bea arrived. She dropped to her knees beside the twisted cockpit, heedless of the grass staining her skirt. Her movements were swift and methodical as she assessed the crumpled figure still strapped into the driver's seat.

Mildred approached the scene, cataloguing details with the detached precision that had served her well in field hospitals during the war. The once-sleek bonnet twisted into jagged metal. Fluids leaked onto the grass—oil, petrol, perhaps brake fluid. The smell of hot metal and burnt rubber saturated the air.

But it was the stillness of the driver that told the story most clearly. Captain Mallory's head lolled at an angle no living neck could maintain. Even through the cracked goggles and blood-streaked leather helmet, it was evident that his face had impacted something with tremendous force.

Dr Marsh straightened up, her expression grim but professional. She met the questioning gaze of the circuit official who had arrived panting, at her side. A small shake of her head was all that was needed.

"He's gone," she said simply. "Broken neck. Death would have been instantaneous."

The official closed his eyes briefly. "I'll need to inform Mr Hartley. And the police."

"I'm here." Kent stepped forward, producing his warrant card. "Detective Inspector Kent, Scotland Yard. I was attending the event."

The official's relief was palpable. "Thank God. We need to secure the area, sir. And the body, of course."

Kent nodded, already surveying the scene with the methodical attention Mildred had observed in him during previous investigations. "No one touches anything until we've had a thorough examination. Dr—?"

"Marsh. Verity Marsh." The doctor rose, brushing ineffectually at the grass and oil stains on her skirt. "Circuit physician. I served with the Queen Alexandra's Imperial Military Nursing Service during the war."

"Field hospital experience?" Kent asked.

"Ypres and the Somme."

Kent nodded, a flicker of respect crossing his features. "I'll need a preliminary cause of death for my report, Doctor."

"Cervical fracture, as I said. Consistent with high-velocity impact. There may be other injuries, but that's what killed him." Dr Marsh glanced back at the broken vehicle. "I'd guess the car rolled at least twice. The human body isn't designed to withstand such forces, even with a helmet."

While Kent continued his conversation with Dr Marsh, Mildred circled the wreckage, careful not to disturb anything but absorbing every detail. The chassis had split near the midsection, exposing mechanical components that had been hidden beneath the sleek exterior. Among the tangle of metal, a particular detail caught her eye.

She moved closer, mindful of the growing pool of fluid. There, among the control linkages: a brake cable, frayed and severed. But the pattern of the break didn't appear consistent with the crash. Rather than a tear, there was a distinct score mark, as though the metal had been partially cut before finally giving way under stress.

And something else; a dark smudge on the metal surrounding the cable. Not oil, which would have been glossy. This was matte, almost like ink or graphite.

Mildred crouched for a closer look, aware of Bea hovering anxiously behind her.

"Mildred," Bea whispered, "do you think it was just a terrible accident? The way the car moved—it didn't seem right, even to me."

Before Mildred could answer, a shadow fell across the wreckage. She looked up to find Kent standing there, his expression carefully neutral but his eyes alert.

"Interesting detail, Lady Ramsay?" he asked quietly.

Mildred straightened. "The brake cable," she said, keeping her voice low. "See how it's severed? That's not consistent with stress failure. There's a scoring pattern."

Kent leaned in, his gaze following her discreet gesture. His eyes narrowed slightly as he took in the dark smudge as well.

"And that's not oil," he murmured. "It's too—"

"Matte," Mildred finished. "Yes, I noticed that as well."

They exchanged a glance fraught with shared understanding. What had appeared to be a tragic racing accident suddenly carried the distinct shadow of something far more sinister.

Their silent communication was interrupted by the arrival of Edwin Hartley, the circuit steward, his precise movements now infused with barely contained distress. Behind him trailed Alf Keating, Mallory's mechanic, his face ashen, his broad shoulders slumped in shock.

"Inspector," Hartley began, his usual crispness frayed at the edges, "this is unprecedented. Captain Mallory was our most experienced driver. His car was inspected thoroughly this morning, as per protocol."

Keating pushed forward, his grief transforming into anger. "It wasn't the car! I checked every bloody bolt myself. Twice! Something happened on that banking—something that shouldn't have."

Kent regarded the mechanic steadily. "We'll need a full statement from you, Mr Keating. And a list of everyone who had access to Captain Mallory's vehicle before the demonstration."

"Everyone?" Keating's face clouded. "That's half the paddock. It's not like we lock the things up. Everyone knows everyone here."

"Nevertheless," Kent insisted, "I need that list."

Hartley intervened, his organisation skills reasserting themselves despite the shock. "I'll assist with that, Inspector. We maintain sign-in sheets for the paddock, and I have a record of Captain Mallory's team members."

THE MYSTERY OF THE FINAL LAP

As the men conferred, Mildred became aware of a flurry of activity at the edge of the gathering crowd. Rae St John was striding toward them, her face a mask of controlled tension. Behind her, a slim man with a camera and notebook, one of the journalists, Mildred presumed, was trying to keep pace while calling questions.

"Miss St John! Lionel Brooks, The Motor. Was there any indication during morning practice that Captain Mallory's car was compromised? Did you observe anything unusual about his line into the banking?"

Rae ignored him completely, making directly for the wreckage. Her eyes swept over the scene with professional assessment before coming to rest on Mallory's still form. Something flickered across her features; not just shock or sorrow, but a flash of calculation that intrigued Mildred.

"This wasn't mechanical failure," Rae stated flatly, addressing no one in particular. "Not the way the car moved. It was as if the brake engaged suddenly on one side."

The journalist, Brooks, was scribbling frantically. "Would you say this calls into question the safety protocols at Brooklands? Or perhaps the maintenance standards of Captain Mallory's team?"

Keating lunged toward Brooks, restrained only by Hartley's surprisingly firm grip on his arm. "You bloody vulture! Don't you dare suggest—"

"That's enough," Kent cut in, his tone leaving no room for argument. "This area is now under police control. Mr Brooks, I'll thank you to step back. Mr Hartley, please begin clearing the circuit of all nonessential personnel. Dr Marsh, if you could remain with the body until the police surgeon arrives."

As the circuit steward began the process of herding away

spectators and press alike, Mildred found herself standing slightly apart with Kent, Bea hovering nearby.

"It wasn't an accident," Mildred said quietly, not a question but a statement.

Kent's expression remained carefully neutral, but his eyes held the particular focus she had come to recognise; the look of a hunter who has just picked up a scent.

"That remains to be determined, Lady Ramsay," he replied, his voice pitched for her ears alone. "But I find it... curious... that the Commissioner was originally meant to attend today's event in my place."

Mildred absorbed this implication. "A coincidence, perhaps."

"Perhaps," Kent conceded. "Though in my experience, coincidences have an unfortunate habit of evaporating under scrutiny."

Bea joined them, her initial shock now yielding to the keen curiosity that made her such an effective ally in their previous investigations.

"Well," she said with forced brightness that didn't quite mask her unease, "I suppose this means our pleasant day at the races has turned into something else entirely."

Mildred met Kent's gaze once more, reading in it the same grim acknowledgment that flickered through her own thoughts. The scored brake cable. The unusual smudge. The precise, targeted nature of the failure.

What had begun as a day of charity and spectacle had veered, like Mallory's doomed machine on the banking, toward a single grim conclusion—the final lap that ended his demonstration run and set the day itself upon a course from which there could be no return.

3

"I'm afraid no one will be leaving the paddock until further notice."

Detective Inspector Kent's announcement fell upon the assembled mechanics, drivers, and officials like a heavy blanket. The initial shock of Captain Mallory's crash had given way to a brittle agitation as the implications began to settle in. Now, with Kent's words, that agitation crystallised into something sharper.

"On whose authority?" demanded a florid gentleman in racing whites and an expensive-looking cashmere jumper. "I have a qualifying run in twenty minutes."

"On the authority of Scotland Yard," Kent replied evenly, "and with the full cooperation of Brooklands management." He nodded toward Edwin Hartley, who stood at his shoulder with his twin pocket watches now conspicuously tucked away, as if time itself had been temporarily suspended.

Hartley stepped forward, his posture somehow even more rigid than usual. "Inspector Kent has my complete support in this matter. All racing activities are suspended until further notice. The Members' Banking will remain closed for examination."

A collective groan rose from the assembled group, quickly silenced by Hartley's glacial stare.

"Timing slips," he continued, reaching into his jacket, "will be distributed to establish each person's whereabouts prior to and during Captain Mallory's demonstration run."

He produced a stack of pale blue cards, remarkably similar to the tea tickets that had been distributed earlier in the day. Mildred, standing slightly to one side with Bea, noted the meticulous attention to detail, each slip was pre-stamped with the Brooklands crest and numbered sequentially.

"Mr Hartley," Kent said, "if you would supervise the distribution of these timing slips, I would be grateful. Each person is to record their exact movements between nine and eleven-thirty this morning, with particular attention to the period immediately before Captain Mallory's demonstration."

A young constable, fresh-faced and eager beneath his regulation helmet, stepped forward with a notebook already open. "Constable Frederick Blake, sir," he announced, his voice cracking slightly with what might have been nervousness or simply youth. "Assigned to Weybridge station. I've been detailed to assist with statements."

Kent nodded. "Very good, Constable. Begin with Captain Mallory's immediate team. Mr Keating first, I think."

As Hartley began distributing the timing slips with mechanical precision and Constable Blake led a still-shaken Alf Keating to a quiet corner to take his statement, Kent turned to Mildred and Bea.

THE MYSTERY OF THE FINAL LAP

"Ladies," he said, his tone softening marginally, "I must ask you to remain within the grounds for the time being. Your observations may prove valuable."

"Of course, Inspector," Mildred replied. "We're at your disposal. In fact, if I might suggest, Lady Beatrice and I could perhaps make ourselves useful while you conduct the formal interviews."

Kent raised an eyebrow, a gesture Mildred had come to recognise as his version of amusement. "I presume you have something specific in mind, Lady Ramsay?"

"A general reconnaissance of the paddock area," Mildred said casually. "People often speak more freely to those they don't perceive as authorities."

"Especially when those people arrive bearing buns," Bea added brightly. "Mrs Thwaite was positively distraught about the accident. I'm sure she'd be glad to contribute to the investigative effort."

Kent considered this for a moment, then gave a slight nod. "Very well. But I must ask you not to disturb any potential evidence. And of course, any information you gather—"

"—will be brought directly to you," Mildred finished. "We're quite familiar with the protocol by now, Inspector."

"Indeed," Kent said dryly. "Sometimes alarmingly so."

As Kent moved away to confer with Hartley about the timing slips, Bea turned to Mildred with the gleam in her eye that usually preceded either a social triumph or an investigative breakthrough.

"I'll fetch the buns," she declared. "You begin the paddock survey. Between us, we'll know more than that poor constable by luncheon."

"Be discreet, Bea," Mildred cautioned. "These people are shaken, not stupid."

"Darling, discretion is my middle name," Bea replied, already moving toward the Clubhouse with a purposeful stride that belied her frivolous reputation.

Mildred suppressed a smile. Beatrice Elspeth Augusta Mortimer had many sterling qualities, but discretion had never numbered among them. Still, her talent for extracting confidences through sheer charm was undeniable and potentially invaluable in the current situation.

Left to her own devices, Mildred began a methodical circuit of the paddock. The space was a warren of temporary stalls, each housing a racing car in various states of assembly or repair. Toolboxes lay open, parts were arranged on clean cloths, and the smell of oil, metal, and high-octane fuel permeated everything.

Most of the mechanics and drivers were gathered in clumps, filling out Hartley's timing slips and speaking in low, urgent voices. Mildred moved among them, not hiding her presence but not drawing attention to it either. A technique she had perfected during her nursing days, when patients often revealed more when they forgot a caregiver was nearby.

Near the storage area at the rear of the paddock, a detail caught her eye; a rack of fuel drums, neatly arranged and labelled. Most bore the standard markings indicating petrol of various grades, but one drum, positioned slightly apart from the others, carried a different designation: "BENZOLE MIXTURE—HIGH CONCENTRATION."

Mildred paused, her attention drawn to the drum not by its label but by its position. It sat among a cluster of containers marked "STANDARD RACING BLEND," yet its warning label was clearly visible. If someone were reaching for the standard blend in haste, they might easily grab the benzole mixture by mistake, a potentially dangerous error, given the different combustion properties of the two fuels.

A thin man in oil-stained overalls was checking items off on a clipboard nearby. His ginger hair stuck out from beneath a cloth cap, and a pencil was tucked behind his ear.

"Excuse me," Mildred said, approaching him. "Are you in charge of the fuel supplies?"

The man looked up, startled. "Yes, miss... I mean, ma'am." He peered at her more closely, recognition dawning. "Lady Ramsay, isn't it? I'm Stringer, parts and supplies clerk." He touched his cap nervously. "Terrible business with Captain Mallory. Just terrible."

"Indeed, Mr Stringer. I couldn't help noticing the arrangement of those fuel drums. Is it usual to store the benzole mixture so close to the standard blend?"

Stringer's brow furrowed as he followed her gaze. "What? No, that's not right at all." He hurried over to the drums, examining the labels with increasing consternation. "These were all properly sorted ten minutes ago, I swear it. I checked them myself when I came on duty this morning."

"Could someone have moved them?" Mildred asked.

"They'd have no reason to," Stringer insisted, now looking genuinely distressed. "We're very careful with the benzole—it runs hotter, you see. Only a few of the cars use it, and those drivers are quite specific about their fuel." He began hastily rearranging the drums, muttering to himself. "Captain Mallory never used the high-concentration mix. Said it was too unstable for the banking."

Mildred watched him work, noting the genuine anxiety in his

movements. "When did you last see the drums correctly arranged, Mr Stringer?"

He paused, thinking. "I'd say about quarter past ten. I was checking inventory before the demonstration runs began." He glanced at her sharply. "You don't think… this couldn't have anything to do with the accident, could it?"

"I'm simply gathering information, Mr Stringer," Mildred replied calmly. "I'm sure Inspector Kent will want to speak with you directly."

As if summoned by his name, Kent appeared at the end of the storage area, his tall figure silhouetted against the paddock lights. Mildred caught his eye and gave a small nod, which he returned almost imperceptibly before continuing his circuit of the area.

Leaving Mr Stringer to his reorganisation, Mildred made her way back toward the main paddock. She had nearly reached the central area when she spotted Bea, true to her word, distributing what appeared to be a basket of fresh buns among the mechanics and drivers. The transformation was remarkable; faces that had been closed and wary moments before softened in the presence of Bea's effervescent charm and the simple comfort of warm food.

Mildred approached just in time to hear a young mechanic, Peter Finch, Rae St John's apprentice, speaking in a low, urgent voice.

"—can't believe it's happened again. Mr Keating was saying just last week that someone had been tampering with spares."

"Again?" Bea asked, wide-eyed, offering another bun. "You mean there have been other… incidents?"

Finch accepted the bun gratefully. "Nothing like this. Just parts going missing, tools being misplaced. But Mr Keating was proper upset about it. I heard him mutter 'not again' when they told him about the Captain's crash."

Mildred filed this information away carefully. Alf Keating's reaction took on new significance in light of previous concerns about tampering.

Bea had already moved on, her basket now half-empty, pausing beside a cluster of journalists. Her charm working more effectively than any interrogation technique.

"—absolute scoop. I was on that footbridge a good five minutes before anyone else. Saw the whole thing perfectly." Lionel Brooks, if Mildred recalled correctly, from The Motor.

"Lucky coincidence, Brooks," another reporter remarked, his tone suggesting he found it anything but.

"Journalistic instinct," Brooks replied smoothly. "Being in the right place at the right time is half the job."

Bea offered him a bun with her most dazzling smile. "How fortunate for your readers, Mr Brooks. Though how dreadful to witness such a tragedy so... intimately."

Brooks accepted the bun with a grateful nod. "All part of the profession, Lady Mortimer. Though I confess, I'd have preferred a triumphant finish to document rather than..." He trailed off, glancing toward the still-visible wreckage on the banking.

"I imagine your photographs will be in high demand," Bea remarked.

"The editor's already wired for them to be sent to London immediately," Brooks confirmed. "But Inspector Kent has temporarily confiscated my camera. Most inconvenient."

Mildred caught Bea's eye, a silent signal passing between

them. Bea gave an almost imperceptible nod before continuing her bun distribution.

As Mildred completed her circuit of the paddock, she observed one final tableau that caught her attention. Near the entrance to the Clubhouse, Victor Pym, the safety cable manufacturer's agent she had heard mentioned earlier, was engaged in what appeared to be a heated exchange with a young clerk. Pym's elegant appearance was somewhat marred by the flush of anger on his face.

"—absolute incompetence," Mildred heard him snap as she drew nearer. "Those documents were to be delivered to Captain Mallory before his demonstration, not after!"

The clerk, a thin young man with spectacles, quailed visibly. "But sir, Mr Hartley said all paperwork had to go through him first, and he was busy with the—"

"I don't care what Hartley said," Pym interrupted. "This delay has cost me—" He broke off abruptly, becoming aware of Mildred's presence. His expression smoothed instantly into a polite mask. "Good morning, madam. I apologise for the disturbance."

"Not at all," Mildred replied coolly. "These are disturbing circumstances."

Pym inclined his head in acknowledgment before turning back to the clerk with a final, low-voiced instruction that Mildred couldn't quite catch. The clerk scurried away, clutching a folder to his chest.

Bea appeared at Mildred's elbow, her empty basket a testament to the success of her mission.

"Well," she murmured, "I've had the most fascinating conversations. Shall we compare notes before reporting to Inspector Kent?"

Mildred nodded, her mind already assembling the pieces of information they had gathered: the fuel drums, Keating's previous concerns about tampering, Brooks's convenient position on the footbridge, Pym's urgency about documents that now would never reach Mallory.

What had appeared initially as a tragic racing accident was developing distinct contours of something far more deliberate and far more sinister.

4

The paddock had settled into a particular quiet that follows a calamity. Not silence, precisely, but a hush broken only by murmured conversations and the occasional metallic clang of tools being set down with exaggerated care. Inspector Kent had established a makeshift interview area in the race officials' tent, where Constable Blake was industriously recording statements with the earnest concentration of youth.

Mildred, having shared her observations about the misplaced fuel drums with Kent, found herself drawn back to the Bentley she had admired earlier; the brilliant green machine belonging to Aurelia "Rae" St John. The car sat in its bay like a sleeping beast, bonnet closed now, tools neatly arranged on a nearby workbench.

Of its owner, there was no immediate sign, but as Mildred approached, a figure emerged from beneath the car's rear end, Rae herself, a smudge of oil across one cheek, a spanner clutched in her gloved hand.

"Lady Ramsay." Rae straightened, her tone neither welcoming

nor hostile, merely acknowledging. "I suppose you're part of the investigation now."

It wasn't quite a question, but Mildred treated it as one.

"Inspector Kent values additional perspectives," she replied carefully. "And I find mechanical problems rather fascinating."

"This wasn't a mechanical problem." Rae placed the spanner precisely on the workbench, aligning it with the other tools. "Not an accidental one, at any rate."

Mildred regarded her thoughtfully. "You sound very certain."

"I am." Rae pulled off her work gloves, revealing hands that were strong and capable but surprisingly elegant. "I've been racing for three years. Before that, I drove ambulances in France. I know the difference between mechanical failure and sabotage."

"That's quite an assertion, Miss St John," Mildred said. "Do you have specific evidence?"

Rae's gaze was direct, assessing. "I saw how the car moved on the banking. The fishtail wasn't consistent with a blown tyre or seized engine. It was a brake failure, sudden and catastrophic."

"Could that have been a maintenance oversight?"

"Impossible." Rae's tone was flat. "Alf Keating is the most meticulous mechanic at Brooklands. And Rex—" She paused, the first hint of emotion crossing her features. "Captain Mallory was equally thorough. He checked every component himself before each run."

Mildred nodded, accepting this without further questioning.

Something flickered in Rae's eyes—caution, perhaps, or simply the private pain of loss. "We were colleagues.

THE MYSTERY OF THE FINAL LAP

Competitors. Sometimes collaborators on testing new components."

"I understand he was scheduled to use a special fuel mixture for today's demonstration," Mildred ventured. "Something about his preferences?"

Rae raised an eyebrow, impressed despite herself. "You've been asking questions. Yes, Rex had very specific requirements. Standard racing blend, never the high-concentration benzole mix. He claimed it made the engine run too hot for the banking, especially in warmer weather."

"And today is certainly warm," Mildred observed.

"Precisely, which is why I find it curious that someone moved the benzole drums this morning." Rae's expression was pointed. "I saw you speaking with Stringer earlier. I assume he told you about the rearrangement?"

"He mentioned it had happened within the last hour before the accident," Mildred confirmed. "You're very observant, Miss St John."

"In racing, observation is survival." Rae ran a hand through her short dark hair, leaving another streak of oil. "The benzole wouldn't have caused the crash directly. Rex would have noticed the difference in engine sound immediately. But it's... suggestive... that someone was interfering with the fuel supply on the same day his brakes failed."

Mildred nodded, impressed by the woman's analytical mind. Before she could frame her next question, however, a cultured voice called from the edge of the paddock.

"Miss St John! My dear, are you quite all right? Such a dreadful business."

The voice belonged to a tall, elegantly dressed woman of perhaps fifty, whose expensive outfit somehow managed to appear both appropriate for a day at the races and conspicuously tasteful in the midst of tragedy. She moved toward them with the measured grace of someone accustomed to being watched, a slight scent of expensive French perfume preceding her.

"Lady Carrington." Rae's greeting was polite but noticeably cooler than her conversation with Mildred had been. "I'm quite well, thank you."

"I've been positively beside myself with worry," Lady Carrington continued, her hand fluttering to the strand of pearls at her throat. "First that dreadful accident, and now I hear the police are questioning everyone. As head of the Ladies' Committee, I feel a particular responsibility for your wellbeing."

"That's very kind," Rae replied, her tone suggesting it was anything but, "but unnecessary. Lady Ramsay and I were just discussing technical matters."

Lady Carrington's gaze shifted to Mildred, a swift assessment taking place behind her carefully arranged expression of concern. "Lady Ramsay. How fortuitous that you're here! Your reputation precedes you, of course. They say you have quite the knack for sorting out... unpleasantness."

"I merely observe," Mildred replied mildly. "And occasionally ask questions."

"Then you must have heard the most distressing rumours," Lady Carrington said, lowering her voice to a confidential murmur that nevertheless carried perfectly. "About tensions in the paddock. Particularly concerning our dear Miss St John."

Rae's posture stiffened almost imperceptibly. "Lady Carrington—"

"Oh, I'm not one to gossip," Lady Carrington continued smoothly, "but in the interest of the investigation, I feel I must mention that Captain Mallory's demonstration slot was originally promised to Miss St John. There was quite the fuss about it last week."

"A scheduling adjustment," Rae said, her voice tight. "Nothing more."

"Of course, dear. And then there was that business with the mechanic—what was his name? Peter?"

"Finch," Rae supplied, her expression growing more closed. "Peter Finch. He's my apprentice now. He previously worked under Alf Keating."

"Yes, that's it. Quite the coup, luring him away from Captain Mallory's team." Lady Carrington's smile was sympathetic, her eyes anything but. "And then those late-night practice sessions on the banking. Most irregular. Mr Sykes, he's our committee photographer, mentioned seeing lights on the circuit well after midnight last Tuesday."

Mildred watched the interplay with interest. Lady Carrington's concern was performative, her insinuations deliberate. The question was why.

"I'm sure Inspector Kent will be interested in all available information," Mildred said neutrally. "Including the activities of the Ladies' Committee."

A brief flash of something—displeasure? concern?—crossed Lady Carrington's perfect features. "We're an open book, I assure you. Now, I really must check on the catering arrangements. This disruption to the schedule has thrown everything into disarray." She touched Rae's arm lightly. "Do take care, my dear. Such dangerous times."

With a final meaningful glance at Mildred, Lady Carrington glided away, leaving behind a faint cloud of perfume and unspoken accusation.

Rae released a breath that was almost a sigh. "I apologise for that performance, Lady Ramsay. Ivy Carrington has appointed herself my guardian angel or perhaps my jailer, since I began racing at Brooklands."

"She seems quite concerned about your reputation," Mildred observed.

"She's concerned about her investment," Rae replied with a trace of bitterness. "The Ladies' Committee sponsors three drivers. I'm the only woman among them, which makes me something of a novelty. Useful for publicity."

"And was there truth in her insinuations?" Mildred asked directly. "About the demonstration slot, the mechanic, the midnight practices?"

Rae considered her for a long moment, as if weighing how much to reveal. Then, with a decisive movement, she reached into her pocket and extracted a pair of driving gloves.

"See for yourself," she said, handing one glove to Mildred. "The evidence of my midnight activities."

Mildred examined the glove carefully. It was well-made leather, supple but sturdy, clearly designed for a woman's hand. The fingertips and palm were lightly dusted with fine metal filings that glinted in the paddock light.

"Filing marks," Mildred noted. "You were working on something metallic. Recently."

"Throttle linkage," Rae confirmed. "For the Women's Ambulance Corps. I've been teaching them basic mechanics, how to maintain their vehicles in the field. We practice at night because most of them work during the day."

"And the Women's Ambulance Corps prefers to avoid publicity," Mildred guessed, remembering her own experiences during the war.

"Precisely. Lady Carrington thinks I'm tarnishing my 'feminine appeal' by getting my hands dirty. The midnight sessions let us work in peace."

Mildred handed the glove back, impressed despite herself by the woman's flinty precision and practicality. "And the other matters? The demonstration slot, the apprentice?"

Rae's mouth tightened. "The slot was originally mine, yes. Hartley reassigned it to Rex last week. Something about a special guest who particularly wanted to see the 'war hero' drive. I was... displeased... but these things happen."

"And Peter Finch?"

"He approached me, not the other way around. Said he wanted to learn from a driver who understood the mechanical side as well as the racing line." A ghost of a smile touched Rae's lips. "Alf was furious, of course. He'd spent months training the boy. But it was Peter's choice."

Mildred considered this new information, filing it away alongside other pieces of the puzzle that were beginning to form a clearer picture. The denied opportunity, the poached apprentice, the secretive night activities—all could be innocent, all could be sinister, depending on the lens through which one viewed them.

"One last question, Miss St John," Mildred said. "If you believe Captain Mallory's crash was sabotage, do you have any thoughts on who might have been responsible?"

Rae's expression hardened. "Half a dozen people had reason to wish him ill. Pym, whose safety cables Rex refused to endorse. Brooks, who was desperate for a sensational story to save his column. Even Ivy, whose investments might have been threatened by Rex's outspoken opinions on profiteering."

She paused, meeting Mildred's gaze directly. "And yes, I'm aware that I'm on that list too. The rival driver with a grudge. But I didn't sabotage his car, Lady Ramsay. I wanted to beat Rex on the track, fairly, not..." She gestured toward the distant banking where the wreckage was still being cleared.

"I believe you," Mildred said after a moment, surprised to find that she did. There was something in Rae St John's forthright manner, her clear-eyed assessment of both machinery and human nature, that rang true.

"That makes you a minority," Rae replied dryly. "But I appreciate it nonetheless."

As Mildred turned to leave, Rae called after her. "Lady Ramsay. Whoever did this understood mechanics. The brake cable, the fuel mix… these aren't amateur mistakes. This was someone who knows cars."

"I'll bear that in mind," Mildred said. "Thank you for your candour, Miss St John."

Walking away from the green Bentley, Mildred found her thoughts racing like the machines that had circled Brooklands that morning. Rae St John presented a compelling figure—capable, direct, and possibly innocent. But innocence, like guilt, could wear many faces, and Mildred had learned long ago that the most convincing performances often came from those with the most to hide.

5

Victor Pym was a man who understood the power of first impressions. Which perhaps explained his conspicuous refusal to look shaken even with the commotion that had blanketed Brooklands since Captain Mallory's crash. He had set up his "Modern Engineering Solutions" display in the Clubhouse with a merchant's pride, spring-cleaned his already immaculate appearance, and now eyed the closed circuit through polished windows as though he might yet find a marketing opportunity in tragedy.

"Lady Ramsay!" His greeting, when Mildred approached, was delivered with the perfect pitch of relief and welcome. "You do bring a sense of calm to the room. It is desperately required after this dreadful morning."

Mildred allowed herself half a smile, noting that Pym's collar was as stiff as Hartley's timetable and that his shoes gleamed in a way that suggested he travelled with his own shoe-boy. He was a man for whom presentation was everything, and sometimes, she reminded herself, presentation hid a multitude of sins.

"I'm not sure I bring calm, Mr Pym," Mildred replied. "But perhaps clarity. At least, I like to think so."

He inclined his head graciously, then turned the conversation with nimble deftness to his exhibit. "You see here the very latest in brake-cable construction, stranded steel, plaited sheath, reinforced anchor barrels. Our firm sets the benchmark. I only wish Captain Mallory had seen fit to champion our efforts. He was most cordial, most professional. Just... resolutely set in his ways."

He flicked open a brochure with a crisp snap that was almost military. "All here. Safety at speed, Lady Ramsay. Surely the future lies here? I mean to reassure the public, especially now. So many rumours. So much to set straight."

"Isn't hindsight a dreadful thing, Mr Pym?" Mildred replied, her voice mild. "Many people were hoping for Mallory's public endorsement. Perhaps yourself included?"

A shadow passed briefly across his face. "Of course. But one cannot force an honest man to speak other than he believes. For Mallory, tradition was virtue and innovation was indulgence. In *una fide*—single faith, Lady Ramsay." He forced a polite laugh. "I must be content with smaller victories."

Before Mildred could reply, Ada Finch, his secretary, hovered at his elbow. Ada's presence was demure but inescapable, her workaday dress immaculately pressed, her eyes darting nervously between her employer and his visitor. She clutched a small ledger, fingers nervously tracing the embossed corners.

"Miss Finch—" Pym acknowledged her with a fleeting flicker of irritation. "Yes?"

She handed over a short document and murmured, "Mr

Hartley requires the safety figures, sir. And the cable test results. Right away, please."

Pym opened his pocket-book deliberately. As he extracted the requested note, Mildred glimpsed small columns of tidy shorthand—entries marked with cryptic initials, numbers, and the occasional symbol. One in particular caught her eye: "M—B, 3gn", a line underscored and bracketed. Pym snapped the book shut, smile fixed.

"Forgive the interruption, Lady Ramsay," he soothed. "The world runs on paperwork. Miss Finch is worth her weight in gold." Ada blushed and tucked the ledger under her arm.

As Pym handed Ada the typed summary, Mildred noted the faint tremor in the secretary's hands and the frown of concern she made no effort to disguise. Ada looked as if she longed to unburden herself of something far heavier than a sheaf of figures, but the nervous glance Pym shot her sent her fleeing instead toward Hartley, back stiff with worry.

Left in reluctant peace with Pym, Mildred returned to the subject at hand. "Was Captain Mallory's refusal much discussed among the manufacturers, Mr Pym? I'm certain the other sponsors would be eager for his approval as well."

Pym's lips pressed together. "Some trades are more patient than others. I believe in the principle of scientific demonstration. One doesn't buy confidence—one earns it." He made an elegant gesture toward the demo cable on his display. "But some of my competitors have been less scrupulous, flinging inducements about as though respect is for sale."

"You'd never offer a modest consideration for... a fair report?" Mildred asked, an arched eyebrow telegraphing both suspicion and amusement.

His jaw tightened before he summoned another forced smile. "Samples, Lady Ramsay! Demonstrations, properly witnessed. That is all my conscience allows. I bear expenses. One must curry attention—never buy it."

From behind the counter, almost as if on cue, a slovenly mechanic with a patch over one eyebrow sidled up to Bea, who had picked the moment to waft through the Clubhouse bearing a basket of currant buns. He cast a wary glance at Pym and muttered from the corner of his mouth: "That one there, last month, he handed Conway from the Gazette an 'independent testing fee' for writing up the cable. Brown envelope and everything. Called it a courtesy, but we all knew."

Bea, all kindness and nothing but, replied, "Thank you, Crib—Mrs Thwaite says it's always bun before tale!" She pressed a warm bun into the mechanic's greasy hand; he grinned and retreated, grease leaving a faint mark on the napkin.

Mildred took her cue. "People do talk, Mr Pym. Especially when money exchanges hands. Such tales do have a way of finding their way up the banking, as it were."

He flushed slightly, then straightened his shoulders. "No one can prove a thing untoward. If some men live by their pens and discover a taste for ham or whisky, what is that to me? I provide samples for proper evaluation, not favours."

Ada Finch, meanwhile, had drifted back towards the pair, casting anxious glances over her shoulder. Mildred caught her gaze and, with that quiet steadiness that invariably coaxed confidences from the reticent, offered a kind word.

"It's never easy, is it, Miss Finch," she said. "Being caught between numbers and notions, and wanting everyone to believe the best."

Ada gave a wan smile. "I mostly wish people would stop shouting. We keep records of everything, Lady Ramsay. Mr Pym is...very particular."

"Quite," Mildred said warmly. "Proper records are a comfort in troubled times. Do you keep one for all the samples you distribute, too?"

Ada hesitated, eyes darting between Mildred and her employer. "Yes, Lady Ramsay. Every cable, every payment, every—" She stopped abruptly as Pym turned an iron stare upon her, and the colour left her cheeks. "Excuse me," she stammered, "I must get the demonstration schedule for Mr Hartley."

Bea, ever timely, offered Ada a consolatory bun. "Fortify yourself, Miss Finch! Nothing beats currants for the nerves."

Ada mouthed a silent thank you and scurried away, leaving Pym to face the two women in an awkward silence.

Pym cleared his throat. "You see, Lady Ramsay, a man tries to build a reputation, and envy calls it corruption. I have nothing to hide."

Bea favoured him with her brightest smile. "And yet even the purest of reputations can attract shadows, Mr Pym. Shall I save you a bun for the inquiry? I suspect Inspector Kent's questions are harder to swallow."

"I hardly think it will come to that," Pym said, though the bravado sounded thin. He busied himself with the alignment of his display.

Mildred considered what she'd learned. "Tell me honestly, Mr Pym—were you present in the paddock, just before Captain Mallory's last run?"

His eyes slid away. "Certainly. I was checking on my display and then delivering figures to Hartley. Miss Finch was with me. We always keep together before demonstrations. One must safeguard trade secrets."

"Of course," Mildred said. "And the samples—?"

"In my locked valise throughout." He gestured to a well-worn leather case beneath the table.

Mildred let the silence spool out. Over Pym's shoulder, Hartley conversed with Inspector Kent, who watched the room like a man who observed not simply persons but the patterns between them.

A sudden, low commotion by the door caught everyone's attention. Crib, the mechanic, was speaking rather too loudly for comfort. "I saw what I saw, and I'll say it again! Brown envelope handed, plain as day. If it was only bun money, then I'm the Prince of Wales!" Hartley was already on his way—order would be enforced.

"Rumour again," Pym muttered, this time unable to muster even the veneer of amusement. "Lady Ramsay, if you have doubts about my firm's integrity, ask the Inspector to audit all we have."

Mildred nodded with grace. "I'm sure the Yard will examine every possible angle. For now, I'm rather interested in something you mentioned. A demonstration later this week? I'd be most keen to attend."

"Excellent," Pym said, visibly relieved to move to less controversial ground. "It's always illuminating to show how things work under observation. I just wish Captain Mallory could have seen for himself how much safer the new methods are. A tragedy... and, if I may say, evidence that progress should not be delayed."

"Perhaps so," Mildred agreed, her gaze sharpening. "Though

sometimes progress hides discomfort better than danger. We shall see what the evidence says."

As she and Bea stepped away, a commiserating glance passed between them. "He's all anxious shine and twitch now," Bea whispered. "You know, I rather think a man as vain as that would die rather than admit a defective product."

"Or kill for reputation," Mildred murmured. "Money and pride are a volatile mix. Add a little envy, and Brooklands could explode."

Bea shuddered. "Let's hope Kent is as thorough as ever. Otherwise Mrs Thwaite will need to bake another dozen buns just to keep us all civil."

They paused in the doorway, watching as Pym's display caught the autumn sun, while the bustle of rival suspicions resumed behind them. The day was no longer orderly, and the Clubhouse no longer innocent, but the search for truth, like a demonstration run, would burn off the chaff soon enough.

Mildred tucked Pym's brochure into her handbag, weighed down by its implied promises, and turned to the next shadowed corridor of truth Brooklands was determined to provide.

6

Brooklands, in the untidy aftermath of tragedy, swelled with rumour. Each rapidly magnified by a scatter of pressmen with pencils poised and eyes as sharp as knives. Through this collective flutter, Lionel Brooks drifted like a silk scarf: light-footed, ever in the right place at the right moment, cultivating an air of watchful detachment.

He materialised at Mildred's elbow with the brisk precision of a well-timed train, camera slung at his hip, portable Corona typewriter lined up beneath one arm like an obedient spaniel.

"Lady Ramsay!" Brooks's smile was dazzling, but it did not so much invite trust as reflect it back onto the beholder, bright and slippery. "Word is, you're the soul of composure in a crisis. A gift this old circus needs, what?"

Mildred regarded his appearance with wry fondness. He always wore a slightly crushed trilby, carried a battered satchel embroidered with press credentials, and sported a waistcoat just rakish enough to suggest that his derring-do was more literary than mechanical. Yet there was a current of restlessness about him, like static in the air before a thunderstorm.

"I believe, Mr Brooks, that you're the one blessed with the knack of... how did you once put it? 'being present whenever disorder chooses to promenade in public.'"

He allowed the compliment with a modest dip of his hat. "What can I say? Fleet Street's bloodhounds are less diligent." He patted his camera affectionately. "I observe, Lady Ramsay. I do not intervene. The pen records, the lens elucidates, but one must never become the story. Terribly bad form."

Almost as a reflex, he thumbed the platen of his typewriter and fished in his coat for a fresh notebook. Mildred was struck, not for the first time, by the near-military discipline of his note-taking: each page clipped in neat columns, with locations, timings, and initials she suspected he had invented for the sake of drama.

Bea appeared at Mildred's side, beaming as always, her hands clasped behind her back in a gesture that made her look both angelic and mischievous.

"Lionel, darling! They say you saw everything from the footbridge. Was it true? Front-row for disaster, as usual?"

Brooks gave her the kind of smile meant for society columns and after-dinner speeches. "My only talent, Lady Beatrice, is selecting the most advantageous vista in any vignette. Fortune favours the mobile. I seldom sit still unless tea is imminent, of course."

Bea tittered. "Some of the other gentlemen from the press suggested you're terribly lucky. Always a few minutes ahead of the crowd…"

"Mere habit," Brooks waved away the implication. "Journalistic nose, nothing more. I make it my business to shadow possibility, which is, after all, the lifeblood of reportage."

A blond, raw-featured young man from The Telegraph, standing close by, snorted. "Or you've a deal with the devil, Brooks. How else do you always know the next place to stand?"

Brooks grinned, unruffled. "No sorcery required, only experience and the willingness to skip a bun for a footbridge."

Bea, always adept at spinning charm from confrontation, intervened sweetly. "Let Lionel have his magic. After all, he's the one who will immortalise us in tomorrow's papers, and I much prefer to be described as elegant and unflappable."

Brooks acknowledged her with a mischievous tilt of his head before dipping it more reverently toward Mildred. "Rest assured, Lady Mortimer, when the chronicles are writ, you shall be the toast of Brooklands."

Mildred, for her part, watched Brooks's hands as he worked: ever in motion, ink staining the pads of his fingers and leaving errant little smears—charcoal on the rubber advance lever of his camera, graphite on the edge of a spare notecard. It struck her as oddly similar to the mark she'd observed earlier on the ruined brake cable: dark, matte, and persistent.

"Busy morning for your pencils," she observed lightly.

He held up his right hand, palm out. "The devil's mark of a chronicler's trade, Lady Ramsay. Graphite in the bloodstream. Couldn't rub it off with carbolic."

"Dangerous occupation, then."

"Why else chase stories rather than write polite tracts about the countryside?" Brooks's eyes twinkled. "Narrative is risk."

As he spoke, Rae St John materialised near the garage, arms folded, listening as intently as a mechanic tuning a stubborn engine. Her pencil, tucked behind one ear, had etched precisely the same dark trace across two fingers. She caught Mildred's glance and, almost imperceptibly, flicked her brow in silent ballet: the ink of truth stains many hands.

Brooks's attention was a restless thing. In the span of their conversation, he completed a sketch of the accident's timeline, jotted two questions for an unguarded mechanic, and captured a surreptitious photograph of the huddle forming around Pym. Bea, in her element, teased him into a small confessional.

"Would you really have rather been anywhere else, Lionel?" she asked, her voice just loud enough for nearby reporters to overhear.

He grew thoughtful. "If I could trade a disaster for an ordinary day, Lady Mortimer, I would. But ordinary days don't sell newspapers, do they? The public wants combustion, spectacle, and human weakness—served, naturally, with a dash of wit."

"You might have missed the crash altogether," she said playfully, "if you'd lingered over Mrs Thwaite's buns."

"My loss, I'm sure." Brooks's voice softened, an echo of regret threading beneath the bravado. "I prefer currants to carnage. But my feet itched—always trust twitchy toes in this game."

Another reporter, a scowling, ink-stained Welshman, cut in. "You're always first out to the bridge when there's action, Brooks. How do you do it?"

Brooks shrugged. "I watched the routine. Noticed which crews moved early, which drivers argued about timings. You'd be surprised what becomes visible if you stop chattering and start listening."

Mildred watched the interplay, filing away every gesture. She could not help but wonder if Brooks's talent for being "first" owed as much to anticipation as to mere luck or perhaps, on a day such as this, he had been looking for something more than a headline.

At that moment, Inspector Kent swept into the Clubhouse with the force of a brisk wind. His gaze flicked over the small assembly of journalists before coming to rest on Brooks. The effect was instantaneous: two scribblers dropped their notepads, another cleared his throat and slunk off to the far end of the terrace. Brooks, in contrast, rose and bowed slightly, as if greeting a fellow chess-player.

"Inspector Kent," he said, "hoping for a statement, or simply a cup of tea?"

Kent raised an eyebrow. "At present, I am hoping for accuracy, Mr Brooks, which is perhaps rarer in the press than honesty among bookmakers."

"Ouch," Brooks replied, unperturbed. "A collegial challenge, then."

"Indeed." Kent's smile was tight. "And since you saw the crash, perhaps you'd care to describe exactly what you observed?"

Brooks launched with the practised ease of a BBC man, spinning out the circumstances of the morning as meticulously as if transcribing a score: "I positioned myself on the footbridge in hopes of catching a panoramic shot for our features. Noticed Captain Mallory's speed was higher on the second lap; the line was cleaner to start, but as he rounded the Members' Banking's steepest pitch, the car suddenly lurched. Sudden deceleration, far more abrupt than a mere skid, then the swerve, the scream of metal, the tumble." He shook his head, genuine sorrow filtering through. "If it was a mechanical fault, it was the most violent I've witnessed at Brooklands."

Kent listened impassively. "Did you see anyone near the car or the drum storage before the run?"

Brooks hesitated. "Plenty of scurrying—the usual suspects. Mallory's mechanic, that supply clerk Stringer, Pym fluttering about with notes and cables, Miss St John pacing. But nothing untoward. I was focused on framing the start-line shot. Frankly, there were more eyes on Miss St John than the pit crew."

Rae, who had come within earshot, interjected with cool restraint, "And yet none of you saw the sabotage, assuming sabotage it was."

Brooks inclined his head, tipping his trilby in his own defence. "People see what they expect, Miss St John. All the world loves a clean race until it's forced to admit something else is at work."

"Or until a story is more valuable than the truth," Rae retorted.

He accepted the rebuke with equanimity. "You wound me, Miss St John, but fairly." Turning to Mildred, he added with just a hint of self-mockery, "I am but a humble chronicler."

As the tension diffused, Bea, never one for silences, produced two currant buns from the seemingly bottomless depths of her reticule, presenting one to each adversary. "A peace offering," she said impishly, "for your respective professions."

Rae rolled her eyes and crunched into the bun. Brooks, always attuned to the needs of an audience, broke his in half, sharing it with Kent, whose eyes glinted as he accepted.

"You see, Lady Ramsay?" Brooks said. "Your companions have an instinct for harmony. Mine is for discord, on the page, of course."

"Yet you both leave your marks," Mildred replied, her gaze returning to the graphite on his fingertips and Rae's pencil. "The public will weigh the evidence in ink, while the case is decided by more resilient means."

Brooks bowed. "The last word to you, Lady Ramsay. Just as it should be."

He moved off, camera at the ready, already drafting tomorrow's column in his head.

As the journalists dispersed, Mildred found herself standing beside Rae, both of them regarding the faint graphite stains that stubbornly refused to be cleaned from either hands or conscience.

"Odd, isn't it?" Mildred murmured. "How truth and falsehood can rub off on us with nothing but the stroke of a pencil."

"Or a cable file," Rae muttered, eyes narrowing thoughtfully.

Mildred tucked that away, letting intuition catch its breath. Around her, the day's routine was reforming, but its essence had altered: trust, suspicion, wit, and the inevitable stinging residue of tragedy all clinging beneath the fingernails.

Onward, then, to the truths that would not so easily wash away.

7

It was the time of afternoon when clouds, rumpled by a sharp autumn breeze, cast patterns across the paddock. The Clubhouse and its gossip were a world away; engines dozed under canvas, and the sharp scent of hot metal now yielded to the earthier perfume of grass and spilled oil.

Alf Keating stood by the battered remnants of Captain Mallory's car, twin streaks of grief and effort cutting through the grime on his cheeks. He was a big fellow, broad in the shoulder and thick about the waist. Far from the dapper breed of racing driver that drew photographers, yet there was a slow purpose to the motions of his hands. He wiped a rag along the edge of the broken bonnet, not with the reverence of a mourner but the anxiety of a craftsman whose reputation lay in ruins.

Inspector Kent had given notice: each paddock member would be questioned privately, but for now, the scene remained Alf's domain, fringed by a respectful distance. Mildred watched the mechanic from a short way off, gathering herself for the task. He'd lost someone; she knew the look and the heat of it. She approached softly.

"Mr Keating," she said. "Would you mind if I asked a few questions? I won't take much of your time."

Alf's only response for several seconds was to tug at his left cuff; a mechanic's habit, she supposed, or else nerves. She noticed the cuff's ragged edge, marked with faint white spatters. Battery acid, unmistakable, and not the kind one acquired in a sitting room.

He gave her a single look, red-eyed but defensive, as if bracing for scolding or indictment. "Suppose you'll ask anyway, ma'am."

Mildred inclined her head, careful to keep her tone low and almost companionable. "Would you start by telling me about your morning? Did you notice anything about Captain Mallory's car before the run?"

That gave him pause. He looked at the engine again, as though memory might be coaxed from metal. "Looked her over, stem to stern. Nothing out of place, far as I could see. Checked the brake lines twice this morning. More, if I'm honest. She's never once failed on my watch."

He spoke in a flat, almost resentful monotone, but his hand kept drifting back to a battered black tool-drawer, half-ajar by a bench. There was something of the nervous animal about him, always returning to a burrow when frightened.

"Did you touch the spares after you'd finished your checks?" Mildred prompted, following his gaze.

"No reason to." He hesitated, then, under the weight of her silence, amended, "But I always give 'em a look before a big run. Habit."

His gaze fell to his boot. There, almost hidden in the laces, was a crumpled bookmaker's marker. Fluttering in the wind, accusing and pitiful. Habit of a different kind.

THE MYSTERY OF THE FINAL LAP

Mildred recognised it instantly, recalling tales from servicemen in her nursing days. Wagers made in hope, markers paid in desperation. She filed the sight away but kept her attention on Alf's hands, big and rough, now smoothing the rag over the same patch of metal again and again.

Rae St John approached, her figure spare and purposeful, arms crossed. "I gave you that tip on the clutch, Alf," she said, voice level with a jolt of steel. "You checked it?"

He looked at her, wounded and suddenly furious. "Do you think I don't know my job, Rae? It's not the clutch that killed him. Or the brakes! Don't talk as if—"

She cut him off, neither unkind nor apologetic. "Then help us find what did kill him. You notice anything odd near the spares before the run? Or in the drum store? Any stranger about?"

He shook his head, stubborn. "Everyone's always about. It's always a mess before a race. But there—" he pointed awkwardly at the tool drawer. "I keep spares locked up. Only me and Rex ever had the key."

Mildred stepped a pace closer, lowering her tone. "Do you mind if I look?" She extended a diplomatic hand, strong with the steady memory of bandages and broken bodies. He hesitated, but at her nod, opened the drawer with a battered key.

Inside, it was a mechanic's treasure chest: new linings, cotter pins, two pristine cables coiled like silent snakes. Mildred ran a finger along the topmost cable; it was smooth, unused.

"You checked each one personally today?"

"Yes. Before his run, and yesterday at shutdown." Alf paused. "Saw a figure by the tool bench at dawn, now you mention it.

Could've been anyone, light was bad. Thought it was Stringer or one of the boys. Didn't think twice."

She watched a muscle flicker in his jaw. "Why not say so before?"

He met her eyes, and in them she saw the old soldiers, the men who could not speak wounds aloud for fear the words would break them. "Because if there's a saboteur, it means someone here did for the Captain on purpose. Would you want to think that of your mates?" He swiped the acid-marked cuff over his mouth, caught himself, and abruptly turned away.

Bea appeared then, neat as ever, wielding a pair of buns and the sort of cheer that melted wariness. "Thought you might want a bite, Alf. It's not wise to brood on an empty stomach, and if you refuse, I'll simply eat them myself and you'll have no one to blame when there are none left at tea."

He managed a short, unsteady laugh. "I wouldn't want to risk that wrath, Lady Beatrice." He took the bun, set it beside him, and managed a gruff: "Thanks."

Mildred gave him a little respectful space and tried a gentle question. "You and Captain Mallory, good working relationship, was it?"

Alf's breath caught. He gripped the edge of the worktable, and when he finally spoke, his voice was rough. "Best chap I ever knew. Treated his team decent—even joined us for a pint, which most fancy blokes wouldn't. Trusted me with his life on the track. Gave my wife roses on our anniversary, would you believe?"

"I would," Mildred whispered.

He shook his head, as if still unable to process the magnitude of loss or perhaps the enormity of suspicion devouring the paddock. "Reckon I've let him down, the end of it. What sort of man lets someone slip something under his nose?"

"He trusted you implicitly," Mildred said. "That's not a failing."

Alf's mouth twisted. "Was out early today. Told Stringer I'd double-check the drums and the spares, like always. Only I saw that fancy chap, Pym, poking about when he thought no one was looking. Said he was dropping off a demo cable, but I swear he had keys he shouldn't. Didn't think it mattered, then." He made a hopeless gesture. "Everything's different after, isn't it?"

"It is," Mildred agreed. "But what matters now is what you remember."

Rae, who had lingered, tried not to let too much compassion slip into her voice. "Alf, did you lock away all the spares yourself just before the accident? Any cables swapped, or odd fingerprints?"

A shadow crossed his face. "Left the drawer shut, but must've wandered off when the tea bell went. Could've done better. But I'd have noticed a swap, I think."

"But there are ways clever hands can cover their tracks," Rae said softly. "You know that."

He didn't meet her eyes. Instead, he plucked absently at the bookmaker's marker in his boot, a fidget so unconscious, Mildred was sure it meant something deeper. She nodded at it gently.

"Bad luck with the races, Mr Keating?"

He started, then attempted nonchalance. "We all have our vices, Lady Ramsay. Bit of a flutter. Never wagered more than I could lose."

"But if you owed, say, a sharp collector money, and someone offered to square it up for a little favour...?" she let the suggestion dangle, watching his reaction.

He went stiff, then relented with a long, ragged sigh. "Not for sale, not my dignity. Captain Mallory paid what he could—said a man could lose more than money in a bad bet. Helped me out last month himself, off the record. But I swear I'd never, never risk—"

Mildred rested a hand lightly on Alf's arm; it was all the comfort one could offer, and it steadied him. "You don't need to protest too much, Mr Keating. Your reputation speaks for itself. You were there at dawn to do your duty, and you have explained yourself."

He spoke almost in a whisper. "I'd give anything to take the morning back. Check the cables thrice instead of twice."

Rae placed a hand on his shoulder, silent but firm. "None of us can change what's done, Alf. But we can help find what's true."

A hush fell, gentler now, the wind through the paddock shifting the tent canvas and ferrying voices faint and far. Inside, permission was given to grieve, if only for a moment.

Bea, breaking the spell as always, piped up. "Besides, if Mrs Thwaite's tea is cold before Inspector Kent gets a grip on things, the whole circuit will be in revolt."

The mechanic managed a faint, appreciative smile, then quietly excused himself, taking his bun and moving off to a quieter bench as if the world had indeed shifted under his boots.

Left alone with Rae and Bea, Mildred reviewed what she had gleaned. Alf's loyalty ran deep; his sorrow was raw and real, but his dawn presence near the drums, his anxiety over swapped spares, and his financial troubles all left troubling gaps. He might not have tampered with Mallory's cables, but he could certainly have missed a sign due to circumstance, fatigue, or simple trust.

She turned to Bea, whose gaze was uncharacteristically sober. "Loss drives us all to folly," Mildred murmured. "We mustn't let grief turn to scapegoating."

Bea nodded. "I'll keep ears open in the Clubhouse. If anyone saw anything odd when Alf was away from his drawer, they'll tell me."

"And I'll talk to Stringer again about the drums," Mildred decided. "I trust Alf's hands and heart. But this is a place where many can handle a cable and only a few would know how to cut one without being caught."

Rae watched them both, quiet and grave. "Storm's coming," she said matter-of-factly. "Not just in the sky. Best find a place to stand before it arrives."

And so, as the shadows stretched long across the battered and grieving circuit, Mildred resolved to pursue every thread, mechanic or bookmaker, rival or friend, until the frayed ends met truth. For she knew, as soldiers and nurses and honest men did, that in aftermaths such as these, only a clear conscience would keep the coming night at bay.

8

There are those who dominate a room by sheer volume or force. Lady Ivy Carrington needed neither. She was an orchestrator by nature, conducting the Clubhouse and its jittery inhabitants with a raised eyebrow, the faintest arch of her lips, and a gloved fingertip resting on a string of pearls. She floated from knot to knot, dispensing condolences and infinitesimal smiles, as though tending an orchid house in need of delicate pruning.

Mildred noticed how Ivy's presence re-cast the atmosphere: nervous drivers offered stiff bows, society wives found their voices modulate and soften, and reporters, usually prone to pushing forward at any hint of scandal, found themselves held at bay by the mere promise that Lady Carrington would, at her own pace, "make a statement for the benefit of the press." Even Hartley, firm as a railway signalman, made time to bow and nod as Ivy approached, though he checked his pocket watch with greater regularity in her particular presence.

The Clubhouse, well-appointed and flooded with early afternoon sunlight, had become Ivy's chessboard. On one table, she arranged bowls of white orchids ("from my conservatory at Kew," she assured any ear within reach); nearby, a stack of glossy charity appeal leaflets mingled with the tributes to Mallory, now being collected for despatch to his family. She positioned reporters by the bay window, where the light would flatter both complexion and gravitas. Her tone in addressing them was a masterclass in controlled sorrow, her every sentence balanced on the edge between sympathy and barely veiled irritation that her event had been tarnished by tragedy.

"I cannot begin to account for this terrible misfortune," she repeated to anyone with a notebook or a typewriter. "We at the Ladies' Committee pride ourselves on both the safety and the standards of Brooklands. Every precaution is taken. I have the fullest confidence in the staff and in Captain Mallory's team. This will be investigated, of course." The last words hung in the air, transparent as a veil and twice as hard to pierce.

Bea, who had stationed herself nearby ostensibly to offer the comfort of a currant bun, gave Mildred a sly nudge. "Observe the distribution of bouquets and blame, darling. She has hugged Mrs Thwaite, commiserated with Keating, and is about to smother that man from The Sketch with a handkerchief scented vaguely of heliotrope and threat."

It was true. Ivy directed events with the same finesse she would have used arranging a tableau for the society pages. She knelt to speak with a trembling kitchen maid—reminded her gently to "be strong," pressed a folded pound note into her palm, then drifted away before more tears could dilute the occasion.

The orchestration extended behind closed doors as well. When Hartley delivered the Clubhouse's correspondence for committee attention, Bea, with typical unassailable cheer, sidled up to lend a hand. She came back to Mildred, holding a slim sheaf of documents, brows raised.

"You must see this," Bea murmured, offering a well-folded paper. "Tucked between the advertisements for afternoon teas and cordials, the risk assessment for today's event."

Mildred read quickly. The ordinary boilerplate, liability for personal belongings, insurance against fire and flood, was there, but one clause was circled in pencil:

'Given the inevitably hazardous nature of motor racing, an accident or fatality cannot be regarded as improbable, and all measures are to be made for crowd control and reputation management in the event of such an occurrence.'

"If that doesn't chill the blood," Bea whispered, "I don't know what does."

Mildred's brow furrowed. She glanced at the addendum: *Note: should any participant or visitor with prominent political or financial standing be implicated, consultation with committee patroness to precede all public statements.*

"At the very least," she murmured, folding the paper and slipping them discreetly into her reticule, "it promises that Lady Carrington is every inch the strategist."

Bea cocked her head as Ivy swept past, in conference now with her committee secretary, Maudie Knowles, an ever-flustered woman clutching a formidable clipboard bedecked with colour-coded ribbons.

"They say the Ladies' Committee handled all fuel orders as well. 'To assist', of course—Hartley supposedly had his hands full with the entries and timings." Her eyes were mischievous. "Possible, don't you think, that a certain influential hand was more involved than she cares to let on?"

It would have been easy to dismiss, if not for the next tidbit that arrived in a whisper: the Ladies' Committee had signed off on the fuel and spares order requisitions, in Ivy's own hand. That information, filtered through Mrs Thwaite's kitchen network and confirmed, by chance, by a footman with excellent ears, solidified the sense that Lady Carrington's fingerprints marked every aspect of today's event.

The more subtle moves were revealed in passing. Ivy consulted quietly with Victor Pym near the window, her gloved hand resting lightly on his forearm, a gesture Mildred knew from the drawing rooms of London: a word in private, a promise, a warning. Pym listened intently, then retreated with a forced smile, his secretary Ada trailing behind, looking rather as if she might faint from the strain.

Later, in the corridor off the main hall, Mildred was drawn aside by a young woman from The Sphere, her dark bob under a neat cloche. "Lady Ramsay, may I have a word? Off the record, I promise."

They stepped into an alcove, where the roar of conversation faded to a manageable hum.

"There's a rumour—several, really." The young reporter's voice was pitched low and urgent. "They say Lady Carrington's influence reaches beyond the committee room. That she's privately invested in Mr Pym's engineering company. That she steers sponsorship and favours to certain drivers, Miss St John in particular. And that wherever she goes, her photographer is within arm's reach."

Mildred recalled the slender, eagle-eyed man with greying temples who had floated on the periphery of Lady Carrington's party all morning, an expensive camera across his chest. Rollo Sykes: committee photographer, reputed to do private portraiture as well as record the committee's charitable works.

THE MYSTERY OF THE FINAL LAP

The reporter pressed on. "If that's true, then she has every reason to control the narrative, especially now. There's talk about how swiftly her committee swung into action after the accident and who was permitted to speak, and who wasn't."

Mildred nodded thoughtfully. She'd seen as much herself. The kitchen staff and mechanics were being gently nudged away from reporters; those willing to speak were gently "escorted" to safer pastures, and only the committee's official line was permitted in public.

Returning to the main room, Mildred found Ivy ensconced on a velvet settee, a small cluster of notables at her feet. She was commenting on the value of caution—"We must safeguard the reputation of Brooklands, for the sake of the sport, the sponsors, and the memory of the departed. Anything less would be an insult to the very ideals Captain Mallory cherished."

It was said with complete conviction, yet Mildred could not help but see the calculation behind every word.

As the crowd rearranged itself, Bea returned, feathers quite unruffled. "I ran into Rollo Sykes by the side corridor. He's never more than two paces from Ivy. I wondered innocently whether his shots of Miss St John were for the committee yearbook or for something more... exclusive. He blushed and nearly dropped his camera."

"Did you hear what was in the box marked 'Personal' on Ivy's desk?" Mildred asked.

Bea nodded. "Private correspondence. Locked. Only Maudie Knowles has the other key, and she's so anxious she might well give it up for a slice of sticky bun."

"Ivy has orchestrated this entire day," Mildred said quietly. "From fuel orders to public statements. If something was meant to happen, or not be found out, it would have been easier beneath her umbrella than under Hartley's administration."

Bea frowned, realising the implication. "A woman like Ivy... she always looks further ahead than anyone else in the room. Perhaps even further than she ought."

As the afternoon wore on, the subtle pageantry continued. Lady Carrington allowed Mrs Pruett's tea to be delivered over protests, personally pressed a cup into Inspector Kent's hand—"You must keep up your strength, Detective, for the sake of us all"—and all but directed the trickle of information flowing to the police.

Ivy's management extended, it seemed, to every corner but one: the little group comprising Mildred, Bea, and, for a moment, Rae St John, who had slipped in at the edge.

Rae nodded a reserved greeting, watching the committee with a gaze that could chill steel. "She offered me an 'advisory' post on the committee last month," Rae said quietly, "conditional on never speaking to the press without her approval. Said it was for the good of female advancement in the sport."

"Did you accept?" Mildred asked, eyebrow raised.

"I told her I was a driver and a mechanic, not a marionette. She suggested I might enjoy an easier life if I revised that view. Since then, Sykes's camera has been on me at every practice. Plenty of prints, but none shown at the Clubhouse. Funny, isn't it?"

"Not funny, no," Mildred said. "Or perhaps not in the way she intended. It's a form of insurance."

Rae inclined her head. "Against what, I wonder?"

"That," Mildred murmured, "is precisely the question."

As the daylight lengthened and the Clubhouse filled with the hush of aftermath, Mildred surveyed Lady Carrington from across a field of orchids, leaflets and subtle, silken schemes. Ivy smiled, as unassailable as the banking, yet no embankment is truly invulnerable, and even the deepest roots can sometimes be exposed.

Later, as Mildred made her notes for Kent, she paused on a phrase that had surfaced in more than one whisper: "Nothing happens at Brooklands unless Lady Ivy means it to." The focus, for now, was on the accident. But she could not shake the sense that, should the threads be tugged in the right order, Lady Ivy Carrington's careful web might reveal more than she ever intended or dared to imagine.

9

In a cold, clear light that made every blade of grass stand sharply to attention, the outlines of Brooklands seemed etched anew, as if the shocks of the day had recalibrated everyone's vision. It was not yet three, but time had warped, compressed by anxiety, stretched by memories and speculation. Amid the murmurs, two figures stood at the paddock's edge, intent not on gossip but on geometry, pace, and the intractable mathematics of truth.

Edwin Hartley, twin pocket watches glinting, waited with military patience for Lady Mildred Ramsay and Inspector Charles Kent. Mildred noticed, as she approached with Kent, that the corners of Hartley's moustache were tighter than usual, his version of wringing hands. For Hartley, order was comfort; and order, today, had been smashed.

"Thank you for indulging us, Mr Hartley," Mildred greeted him.

"Ladies and gentlemen must be safely satisfied with integrity, Lady Ramsay," Hartley replied without a hint of irony. "If we are to understand how things unfolded, we must follow the track precisely."

He led them first to the warm-up area, each step purposeful. "Captain Mallory's car emerged from here, yes. According to my watch, ten forty-nine precisely." He raised his right-hand pocket watch, then cross-checked with the left. "I was here. I always record the start."

Kent, notebook at the ready, nodded. "And the footbridge?"

"We shall proceed." Hartley's boots sounded neat on the gravel, unhurried, exact. "From the warm-up enclosure, Mallory drove past the garage stalls, then rounded the paddock's eastern edge. It's a one-minute drive at race speed, perhaps two at today's pace." He stepped off the distance, consulting the watches at both ends. Kent followed with a long stride; Mildred kept in step, quietly noting sightlines as they walked, a nook where one might hide, an alcove where hurried hands could switch a fuel drum.

The footbridge was the next station, arching above the Finishing Straight. From its centre, one commanded a view of most of the circuit and the rear paddock lanes; it was both grandstand and bottleneck for spectators, runners, and reporters seeking a story's vantage.

"Several witnesses placed Mr Brooks here moments before the crash," Kent remarked.

Hartley's mouth was a taut line. "Brooks was a regular at the bridge. A creature of habit, you might say."

Mrs Pruett, the circuit's long-serving tea vendor, hovered nearby in her smock, a willow-pattern jug in hand. On seeing Mildred, she hurried over, cheeks pink in the wind, ready to offer reassurance or rumour as required.

"I served that Brooks fellow a cup just before the accident, Lady Ramsay! Down there by the rail—oooh, nearly scalded him as he jostled into position," she explained, pride and distress mingled in her voice.

"Do you remember the time, Mrs Pruett?" Kent asked gently.

Mrs Pruett fished a battered wristwatch from her apron. Its cover engraved with a dartboard motif, the glass cracked through the seven. "Ten minutes before the noise, I'd say. But I'm afraid my clock runs a trifle slow."

"Fifteen minutes, by my reckoning," Hartley confirmed, eyes flicking to his watches. "Allowing for Mrs Pruett's charity with the buns."

Mildred smiled kindly. "Thank you, Mrs Pruett. That confirms Mr Brooks's story, at least for part of the timeline."

Mrs Pruett, appeased, bustled away, retiring to her urn.

A boy messenger in short trousers loitered by the steps, pushing a battered bicycle. Sensing an audience, he straightened. "'Scuse me, sir… ma'am… was I needed?"

Kent nodded encouragement. "Your name, lad?"

"George Lane. I run errands for the drivers, fetching whatever's needed. Saw Miss St John by the banking just before the crash. She'd nicked a spanner from the box and dashed toward the rail. Couldn't say what she was up to. Seemed in quite a rush."

Hartley nodded. "Miss St John… timing suggests she was at the far side of the banking, not the start-line, just before the incident. She moves quickly, but the circuit's not small. Three minutes from paddock to far rail, if brisk."

Mildred clocked the timelines in her mind. Brooks had been on the footbridge, served tea (with a possible five-minute ambiguity thanks to Mrs Pruett's clock). Rae could have been at the rail or between stops, according to George. The tightness of the minutes, a scurry here, a detour there, became suddenly all-important.

Back at the press tent, Hartley gestured upwards with the hand that held his left watch. "From this tent, across the gravel, one minute to the bridge at a clip; from the garage row, slightly longer."

Inside, reporters were now reconstructing events in urgent, overlapping voices. Mildred caught fragments as they passed. "Couldn't have been there, saw him by the rail, pushed through—" She recognised the shifting of timelines, each adjusted subtly to favour its protagonist.

Hartley, relentless and cool, kept on. "I make the window for a saboteur"—he paused just long enough for dramatic effect—"little more than three minutes. From the time the paddock was left unsupervised, to the approach of Captain Mallory, to the crash."

Kent scribbled. "That leaves a handful of opportunities. None impossible, all requiring certainty and daring." He looked at Mildred, his gaze a challenge and an invitation.

Mildred folded her hands over her reticule, considering. "One could, in theory, slip away from the press tent, dart through the crowd, reach the paddock, and return, all in three minutes, perhaps less if one didn't mind sweat or stares. But for someone unaccustomed to such haste, or unfamiliar with the shortcuts... much trickier."

She paused, letting her gaze settle on the trees bordering the gravel walk, the bench shielded by Hartley's orchid pots, the stretch of shadow where a figure might easily wait unseen.

From across the field, Mildred caught sight of Bea, who had taken up her own post near the Clubhouse, flirting information from committee secretaries with a bun in her hand and a quip on her lips.

"Suppose someone did use that window," she asked quietly. "What would be required? Confidence. Nerve. A knowledge of when the eyes of others, Hartley's, the press's, Rae's, were most reliably averted."

Hartley showed a faint hint of approval, glancing to Kent. "You draw a tidy net, Lady Ramsay." He pocketed his left watch but kept the right out, its face shining steady.

Kent's smile was oblique. "And you, Mr Hartley, will be the one to tie the knots."

There was a silence, not unfriendly, as the trio stood together. Mildred gazed at the circuit stretching away, its lines curved and clean, its surface now so freighted with memory and motive that she could almost see the day's events scarred upon it.

She thought again of Alf Keating, visible in the pit row, head bowed over a cable. Of Pym, pacing his little territory near his demonstration case, Ada Finch at his heels. Of Brooks, dramatic and smiling, adjusting his camera even after all else was chaos. Of Lady Carrington on her velvet throne, invisible threads running from her gloved hands.

Evidence, thought Mildred, was not numbers or even hours, but line and opportunity, the geometry of intent. Motive lived in instants.

With that, Hartley bowed and departed, summoned by a persistent Maudie Knowles, who approached brandishing a pile of telegrams and a schedule trembling with fresh amendments.

Kent waited while Mildred watched the sunlight shift on the road. "Well, Lady Ramsay," he said quietly, "shall we compare maps this evening? Mine drawn in untidy ink, yours, if you'll forgive me, in cleaner lines."

She smiled in earnest, something almost light in her chest

despite the day. "Maps are only as useful as the compass that reads them, Inspector. Let's see if the points connect."

A gust of wind lifted the Union Jack atop the Clubhouse into brilliant movement. For a brief moment, all of Brooklands seemed paused—three minutes between questions and answers, between possibility and certainty.

A net was forming. Knots were being tied.

And somewhere, Mildred was nearly sure, the smallest slip, the lightest mis-placement of a drum or a tool or a moment, would prove enough to reveal murder done in the name of speed.

10

Mildred paused at the threshold of the Brooklands press tent, lips set in a thoughtful line as she observed the peculiar rituals of the newsmen. At first sight, the enclosure might have passed for any other field encampment: battered folding tables, a kettle hissing on a camp stove, and the ceaseless click-clatter of typewriter keys. Yet here, the air felt restive. Taut with rumour and rivalry, jostling with swift hands, keen eyes, and, underlying it all, the faintest hint of conspiracy.

Her friend Bea had already begun her familiar campaign. With the effortless confidence that came from years of drawing rooms and society committees, Bea circled from group to group, basket of currant buns aloft, bestowing both pastry and warmth with true intent. Mildred watched, inwardly amused at how quickly the mood shifted when faced with comfort and kindness. The hum of voices dropped, sharp-toothed asides softened, and notepads were set aside in favour of sticky fingers. Even the gruffest reporter from The Illustrated London News managed a shy smile after a third helping.

From her vantage point , Mildred saw more than indulgence; she saw calculation. Brooks, sleek as ever and permanently installed at the central table, received Bea's offering with a flourish, treating her to a story and a wink. Around him, younger reporters hung on every word, effected either by his reputation or the lingering idea that he might offer a sliver of insight or a crumb of his bun.

A gentle swirl of conversation rose as tongues loosened. "Brooks is always first to the scene," confided one red-nosed man to another. "Don't know how he does it—footbridge or finish line, he's always there for the shot."

"Luck, or a tip-off?" someone else replied. "Fleet Street never did run on hunches alone, if you gather my meaning."

Mildred drifted closer, keen to catch the mood. She took up a cup of tea at the edge, watching how Brooks soaked up the admiration and measured envy with practised charm. He was simultaneously the life of the tent and its principal object of speculation. Admired for his sharp eye and resented for seeming always to be one well-polished shoe ahead.

Bea made her rounds, casually steering the topic from Bath buns to more pointed matters. "Everyone claims to have seen something, but which among you was, in fact, in the best place?"

Brooks grinned, feigning humility. "One never quite knows, Lady Beatrice. I like to think Providence smiles upon the observant. It's really a matter of finding the right angle, both for the lens and the story. What's a morning's catastrophe if not a story waiting for the right punctuation?"

A chorus of good-natured scoffs met this, but Mildred noted the undertone: certain of the men had clearly nursed grievances longer than their cups. Envy was currency among those who traded in words and secrets.

THE MYSTERY OF THE FINAL LAP

While Bea worked her diplomatic magic among the gathered crowd, Mildred's attention turned to the sallow, anxious figure of Miss Ada Finch. The young secretary stood at the margin, wringing her hands and casting nervous glances toward the Pym display and the committee table. Mildred remembered her own first forays into the pressure-cooker of public scrutiny—Ada's discomfort was all too familiar.

Seizing a lull, Mildred offered Ada a seat and softened her posture with a smile. "Miss Finch, you look as though your nerves have been tested more than a new clutch cable."

Ada tried to laugh but only managed a small sigh. "Mr Pym wants these reports sent up to the committee room and the press tent," she murmured, indicating a thin folder clutched to her chest. "And there's talk, well, whispers, that an anonymous letter was sent to Captain Mallory. I had to use the communal typewriter in the Clubhouse for a draft Mr Pym dictated—a note of, oh, professional courtesy he called it, meant to be gentle advice. But I left the machine for a moment and, well, anyone could have used it, really. I do feel rather wretched about it."

Mildred's interest sharpened, though her expression betrayed nothing but sympathy. "You typed it unsigned, I take it?"

Ada nodded. "He said it was less confrontational that way. No name, no need for awkwardness. Just a polite warning to be more diplomatic about upcoming safety improvements. I didn't mean to cause any trouble, Lady Ramsay, honestly."

Mildred squeezed her hand encouragingly. "None of this is your fault, Miss Finch. All manner of traffic runs through committee pigeonholes and public machines. Did you see anyone else by that Underwood while you were away?"

Ada hesitated, brow knotted. "Yes, Mr Sykes, the committee photographer, and I think Mr Brooks for a bit; he often drafts releases there. And any number of the driver's assistants; it's a busy corner. The carbon copies were muddled when I came back. I can't be certain my draft wasn't moved or duplicated."

Bea slid by with a warming smile and an extra bun, distracting Ada just long enough for Mildred to excuse herself. She made for the tent's battered writing desk, a relic of greater order now smeared in carbon and cigar ash. There she rifled through the outgoing correspondence, soon finding what she sought: a carbon copy, anonymous and impersonal, of the letter Ada described. Its tone was mild, but to an anxious reader could well mutate, especially if altered, into warning, or even threat.

Dear Captain Mallory, A word in the professional interest — there are those who would appreciate discretion regarding new safety enhancements and suppliers, given the public's skittish temperament. We trust your judgement, as ever, that what's best for the circuit is also best spoken considerately. Respectfully...

Mildred folded it into her reticule. If this note was harmless, another draft could easily bear more malice. And the communal typewriter's presence, an open door for mischief, set her mind at a new angle.

She returned to the hubbub. Brooks was now fielding questions from two younger men about his precise movements before the crash. Mildred noted, as she had earlier, the graphite stains on his fingers; innocuous enough for a chronicler, but in the context of tampered cables, entirely ambiguous.

Near the entrance, a group of runners discussed who'd fetched whom to the rail, and at what time. Everyone seemed keen to clarify their own whereabouts, to both alibi themselves and claim the headline.

A sudden commotion in the far corner drew Mildred's attention. Mrs Pruett, tea urn in one hand, had cornered Inspector Kent. "I served Mr Brooks here, a full ten minutes before the crash! But my watch, it does run a little slow, mind."

Kent, stoic and patient, carved a line through the contradictions, taking notes as stories clashed and converged.

When the Inspector approached, Mildred fell in beside him, matching her stride to his. She relayed what Ada had told her, careful to stress the chaotic accessibility of the typewriter. Kent frowned, then nodded to the letter Mildred produced.

"Anyone could have mimicked this format and tone,' Kent observed. 'Pym's hand, Brooks's type, Sykes's convenience—each as plausible as the other. And unsigned, it's as useful as an alibi without witnesses."

Bea, joining them, tugged Mildred's sleeve. Quietly: "The talk now is that Captain Mallory had warning, even threats. If anyone could have written a sharper note in Ada's style, pushed it alongside hers, and left it to be found—"

Mildred's gaze sharpened. "And then made use of the confusion as a screen for something far worse."

"That's just it," Bea whispered. "Every cheeky rival, every nervous sponsor, they're all a little more wary now."

"As are we," said Mildred, clutching her handbag tight as a shield.

Night crept into corners. The press tent swelled with competing versions. For Lady Mildred Ramsay, the bylines and the buns had done their work—opening mouths, loosening stories, and introducing a shadow: the anonymous typewritten warning, and with it, a clear sense that every easy tale at Brooklands might conceal a blade.

She would turn her attention next to those who used words as deftly as tools, and see, too, what else that busy communal typewriter had quietly, fatefully, produced.

11

The Brooklands afternoon had lowered by a degree, the light pin-sharp, as if the world itself had paused for examination. Mildred found herself once again at the epicentre of activity in the paddock, this time where science met suspicion, and where, for once, the clatter of engines had given way to the quieter music of questions.

Kent was already at work. He stood under the awning near the mangled remains of Captain Mallory's car, holding the scored brake cable between thumb and forefinger. Onlookers buzzed with interest as Kent wiped a pale cotton swab along the jagged edge of metal, turning it this way and that in the light.

"A moment, if you please," he called to a cluster of mechanics hovering at his elbow.

They shuffled, a little embarrassed, a little eager, while Kent uncapped a bottle of solution borrowed from Dr Marsh's kit. He daubed the cable, then observed a muted, silvery mark where "oil" ought to have produced an unmistakable gleam.

"Well, Lady Ramsay," Kent murmured without looking up, "it seems this is not the usual oil at all."

Mildred considered the residue. The smear was distinctive: not glossy as one would expect from machine grease, but crystalline, almost powdery in the oblique light. She reached out, careful not to contaminate evidence, and sniffed delicately. No petroleum scent, no burnt tang. Rather, something cleaner, more neutral, reminiscent of the faint haze that sometimes lingered over schoolroom desks in exam season.

One of the older mechanics, a Cornishman named Selleck, peered closer, shaking his head. "That's not oil. That's graphite, Inspector. We use the dust for drafting, sometimes for steering-boxes, key-slots, and—" He hesitated, searching for words. "Lock springs, too."

The younger lads looked at the cable as if it might combust anew. "What's graphite doing there?" one muttered, still wary.

"It polishes smooth as silk on a threaded bolt," Selleck reasoned, "but it's not natural for a brake cable in that spot. Someone's been... well, doing more than a casual sweep."

Kent turned, eyes hooded with thought. "Would anyone have left such a residue by mistake?"

Mildred could see from the shifting glances in the small crowd the discomfort this question raised. Accidents belonged to Fate—deliberate marks to men. "Pencils," she murmured. "Could it be from the fine lead of a drafting pencil?"

"Could be," Selleck shrugged, "but why bring it to the cable itself, unless you were tampering—"

He was cut off by the arrival of Mr Smith, president of the Motor Club, resplendent in a double-breasted jacket and still smelling faintly of cigars. He interrupted briskly. "If it's graphite you're after, I can show you a pound of it in the Club supply cabinet. It's used for lampblack in the exhaust test, and the stuff gets everywhere. Lads track it on their boots, stains your shirt sleeves if you're careless."

Hartley arrived, timing slips arrayed like a hand of cards. "Anyone with a lock to polish could have had the dust on their fingers, Inspector." He looked from Kent to Mildred, sober-faced. "And Smith is right. We keep a pot of lampblack on the shelf past the changing rooms. Never locked. Never empty, either."

Mildred, attentive, let her eyes flicker from the cable to the mechanics, then to the knot of suspects or personalities she'd come to know: Victor Pym, standing stiff by his demonstration stand; Aurelia Rae St John, hands folded and lips drawn tight; Lionel Brooks, notebook dangling from his fingers and his camera slung across his chest like a talisman.

She felt the electric hush that follows a crucial card being drawn: whose hand had left graphite on that cable, and in what spirit, carelessness or cunning?

She stepped to Kent's side and spoke low, "Graphite on the brake cable's cut. Equally possible: a pencil, a camera shutter, a typewriter ribbon spool, lampblack... all common currency, all scattered hands."

Kent nodded, appreciating her deduction.

They invited the three principal suspects—Pym, Rae, Brooks—forward for a short, informal interview beside the open bonnet. Pym came first, smooth as ever, but with a sallow tint to his cheeks that had not been there at lunch.

"Mr Pym," Kent began, "you work in cables, sheaths, engineering—ever come into contact with graphite powder or similar material today?"

"No more than usual," Pym replied, schooling his features into confidence. "It's everywhere in this business—stopwatches, cable housings—it helps when assembling prototype runs." He cast a sidelong glance at Mildred, then at the mechanics, as if already calculating which way responsibility might drift.

Rae listened, expression blank as tarmac. "Anyone in this paddock could have dust on their hands. I used pencil for the fuel chart," she said, holding up two neat, oil-smudged hands. "Try to scrub it off, you'll be here till next week."

Brooks interjected with mock self-pity. "Am I to be frisked now? My pockets are lined with pencil shavings, cost of the trade. Graphite's the writer's perfume, Lady Ramsay. And I write more than these chaps drive."

Even Rae's lips twitched, just perceptibly.

"Yet graphite isn't the only explanation," Mildred mused for the group. "Typewriter ribbons use it sometimes. And I understand lampblack is prevalent, Mr Smith attested as much. Not to mention the carbon powder that lines the edge of many old camera shutters." She glanced, pointedly, at Brooks's battered Leica. "Can you account for where your camera has travelled today?"

Brooks was unflappable. "Through mud, sun, Reporter's Row, and the Club bar," he recited. "But never, I assure you, into a brake drum."

Pym, near to trembling now, stiffened further under the scrutiny. "I should think you might look closer to the garages by the footbridge, Inspector. Cables are coiled for display all day. Anyone could have run a finger down one to test the tension, picked up dust that way."

Rae, refusing to be defensive, shrugged. "Or perhaps the Club's own supply is the culprit."

Hartley stepped up with prosaic reassurance. "The lampblack pail is always open. Staff use it on everything from friction blocks to doorknobs. If you dusted a surface in this place, you'd find graphite, or something much like it, on a hundred hands in the first five minutes."

Kent swept the gathering with a penetrating gaze, weighing truth amid the shifting sands of plausible deniability.

Mildred stood a moment, considering the possibility that the very ubiquity of the material was itself the greatest shield for the saboteur. No fingerprint; no damning spot; just the echo of an intent, lost in the muddle of honest work and sly malice.

A ripple went round as Brooks, always happiest in the spotlight, cracked a joke to ease the tension. "If the solution's in the dust, perhaps we should all take our shoes off at the door and see who leaves a mark."

There was laughter. Even Hartley coughed, the corners of his mouth nearly curving. But Mildred saw which laughter ran cold, whose eyes scoured the others for reaction. The game of suspicion was on.

Pym excused himself quickly, glancing back at Mildred as if she might read a verdict from the set of his shoulders. Rae, arms folded, gave Mildred a short nod of genuine respect before returning to her grease-smeared notebooks. Brooks, twirling a pencil and grinning broadly, retreated behind his typewriter, muttering about graphite being far less grim than blood.

Kent leaned toward Mildred, voice pitched just for her. "A clue that stains every hand is hardly a clue at all, Lady Ramsay."

"But if we meet the right hand with the right timing," she whispered back, "even the commonest dust might tell a story."

She watched as the group dispersed: Brooks already drafting fresh copy; Pym, face shadowed, deep in whispered consultation with Ada Finch; Rae, stonily resigned but still observing everyone's movements. She marked it all for later. Lampblack, pencils, shutter grease, so many routes to dust, but only one, she felt sure, to deliberate harm.

Dusk had begun to gather, its haze pulling shadows longer over the open track. Mildred promised herself she would not be distracted by prettily painted possibilities. Beneath every layer of graphite and lampblack lay intent, and finding the hand that had applied it to Captain Mallory's cable would require clarity. Perhaps, in the end, a clarity as fine and grey and elusive as the dust itself.

12

Evening's long shadows brought a hush across Brooklands, but within the Clubhouse, intrigue flowered anew. Mildred, far from weary, felt her energy sharpen as smoke, scandal, and shared fatigue scented the air. Lady Ivy Carrington had posted herself in the lounge like a society column come to life, a vision in dove-grey silk, her ever-present strand of pearls catching the last pink light from the window. Around her, the committee fluttered: secretaries at ready, Maudie Knowles with her clipboard, and, as always, Mr Rollo Sykes hovering, camera at the ready.

"I do hope you can set our minds at rest, Lady Ramsay," Ivy trilled as Mildred approached. "It seems Brooklands is quite abuzz with the most dreadful gossip about Miss St John. I'm told she was seen on the banking after midnight! Terribly improper, even for our new era. One strives for progress, but there really are limits…"

She lowered her voice, inviting Mildred into the confidence of her anxiety. "It would be one thing if she were just another ambitious young man, but Aurelia is supposed to represent a certain standard. Now, of course, some of the gentlemen are murmuring that she 'tests' cars in ways not on the official programme. For the life of me, I cannot see why anyone would undertake such laps under cover of darkness, unless... well, unless it were something unsporting."

Mildred regarded Ivy without blinking. "Rumours thrive on scarcity of facts, Lady Carrington. And darkness makes all cats grey, does it not?"

Ivy leaned in, her eyes alight with the theatrical prospect of scandal. "Well! You will hear it from Sykes, if not from me. He claims to have captured evidence of these clandestine escapades. Was setting up some night-plates for the committee's next calendar—'Orchids by Moonlight,' he called it—when his lens caught what appeared to be a motorcar on the high banking, the silhouette unmistakably feminine behind the wheel. Scandalous!" Her tone suggested that nothing could be more thrilling.

Mildred merely nodded her thanks and signalled for a word with Mr Sykes, who hovered on the edge of a lamp-lit table, one boot nervously scuffing the Turkish carpet. Rollo Sykes was a thin man, nervous as a field mouse but aspiring to the dignity of a hunting cat. His camera hung about his neck like a badge of office; the light glinted off its brass fittings.

He brightened as Mildred hailed him. "Do hope I'm not in the way, Lady Ramsay. The Club is still rather particular about who photographs what." His eyes flickered towards Ivy, acknowledging the pecking order.

"Lady Carrington mentioned your photographs of the banking last night," Mildred said gently, "and the possibility you recorded someone, Miss St John, perhaps, testing the circuit?"

He looked simultaneously flattered and wary. "Ah, well. The committee wanted moonlit atmospheric shots, bit of a challenge, considering the weather, so I tried a few long exposures by the Members' Banking. I left the plate in for a twenty-minute soak, you see, and, well… something moved through the exposure. Most ghostly! I developed it today. The figure… it's not quite clear, but the pose… well, it's enough to get the gossips in a twist."

"May I see it?" Mildred's tone left little room for refusal.

Sykes fumbled in his leather folio and produced the plate, holding it to the light. Indeed, across its grainy expanse there ran a swoop of banking in sepia moonlight, and, etched against the track's curving arc, a dark shape, apparently a car, with a figure at the wheel. Silhouette only, blurred from motion, the head uncovered or hatless, hair cropped close against the skull.

"Could be anyone, really," Sykes murmured, "though the general consensus is that Miss St John is the likeliest candidate. She is, in stature and style, rather unmistakable. Not many lady racers in these parts."

Mildred examined the plate. It was evocative rather than revealing; the scene as much suggestion as record. "You must get more than this into the Society Calendar, Mr Sykes. There's mystery enough for a half-dozen stories."

He shook his head, a conflicted smile on his lips. "Lady Carrington said not to mention this to anyone outside the committee. Reputation, you know. But someone used the darkroom during tea, found the plate out drying and had a good look, I'd wager. Word travels."

"Thank you, Mr Sykes." Mildred handed back the plate. "I promise discretion."

She left him standing, visibly relieved, and headed for the paddock where she'd last seen Rae St John. The workshops were quiet now, tools set aside, and the maths of the day's suspicions had largely been replaced by the arithmetic of tired mechanics calculating the hours until supper.

Tracking Rae down was easy; she never hid in public. The Bentley was open, and Rae was working over her kit, sorting gloves, inspecting gaskets, her posture wary but unhurried. As she lifted a battered black case onto the bench, something metallic glinted among the rest: the badge of the Women's Ambulance Corps, tucked beside her spare goggles and a small roll of bandages.

Mildred smiled, nodding at the insignia. "I see you keep your credentials close, Miss St John."

Rae started a little, then shrugged. "A habit hard-won, Lady Ramsay. You never know when you'll be mistaken for an imposter, especially at this club."

"I heard the rumour," Mildred replied gently, "that you were out on the banking last night. Ivy Carrington is worried for your virtue or her calendar or maybe both. And Sykes claims photographic evidence. Quite a story."

She expected Rae's hackles to rise, but instead a slow, private smile crept across her face. "It's not the first story they've spun about me behind velvet ropes. It won't be the last. The truth is simpler. I was running a series of night drills."

Mildred arched an eyebrow. "For the ambulance service?"

Rae nodded. "The committee prefers that only gentlemen, and select lady patrons, use the formal slots. But the women I train work during the day. They can't afford time off, nor to draw attention. So, we use the circuit when no one will report us."

"And the woman you were instructing—?"

Rae's expression turned resolute. "Isn't mine to betray. She's a widow, working in the town surgery. Her pension's been threatened before. If the Club discovers her name in connection with me, she'd lose her post, and the Ladies' Committee would be only too delighted to see the ambulance initiative fail. They'd rather I smiled for the camera than taught carburettor repairs."

It was a reply of quiet fury, and Mildred recognised the depth of Rae's loyalty. "Your secret is safe with me," she said softly. "And your reserves of patience must be remarkable."

Rae's face softened, the smile real this time. "There's nothing like having to fit oneself to other people's rules to make an athlete out of an otherwise peaceable heart."

"Ivy's not the only one to see shadows where there may be none," Mildred observed. "Mr Sykes's photo could as easily be my brother trying to impress his city friends, or half the young men in the club snatching a thrill."

Rae zipped her kitbag shut with a little more force than necessary. "Shadows are convenient. They make any narrative plausible. But let no one doubt—I was only out to help, not to race, not to sabotage. If I break a rule, it is one with honour."

Later that evening, as Mildred scanned a fresh set of Sykes's developed plates in the Clubhouse's makeshift darkroom, she realised how ambiguous the "evidence" truly was. One exposure in particular, the supposed smoking gun, showed nothing but a half-blurred figure skimming the banking in a low-slung car. The silhouette, while undeniably trim, could on longer reflection, belong to any short-haired driver: a boy messenger, an ambitious mechanic, even a society wife grown restless while her husband dozed.

With a slow, ironic smile, Mildred slipped the plate into her sleeve and returned to the lounge, where Ivy was recounting, for the third or fourth time, the horrors of "midnight laps" to a rapt audience. Sykes scurried in her wake, camera swinging, issuing vague promises to keep plates confidential.

As she passed Bea, who was stirring tea and gathering darts thrown in Ivy's direction, Mildred murmured, "The dark is very powerful in committee circles, darling. Today, I think it covers both sin and virtue."

Bea grinned. "Well, never mind the clock or the calendar—just tell me who's telling the most interesting fibs, and I'll top up your cup."

Mildred, knowing the value of half-seen silhouettes and half-heard alibis, returned to her vigil, feeling the sticky bind of rumour and reputation. In the end, she thought, more was hidden in darkness at Brooklands than any mere driver's midnight lap—ambition, fear, and perhaps the shape of murder itself among them.

But for now, the shadow on the plate was as inconclusive as every whispered story, undaunted by truth, waiting for the right angle before fully revealing itself. The mystery, as ever, ran on.

13

The corridors of the Clubhouse had grown eerily still after nightfall. By the time Mildred and Bea slipped on their coats, most of the guests had dispersed into soft autumn darkness, called away by supper tables or, as in their case, a discreet car sent by Mildred's brother to the family house in Weybridge. Kent and Hartley, both resistant to comfort, remained huddled over paperwork and statements well past midnight, while Lady Ivy disappeared to her dower suite at a riverside hotel ("for the Committee's privacy," she'd trilled), and Rae retreated to digs above the garage with her kit and an unreadable expression.

Sleep for Mildred was shallow, a fog of engine noise and whispers, bun-fuelled anxieties, and the faint trace of graphite in her dreams. At some point, Bea's gentle snoring, drifting from the neighbouring room, offered a bittersweet kind of reassurance: if the world was wrong, at least it still abided by certain human oddities.

Dawn at the Ramsay house broke with sunlight slicing through thin curtains. Breakfast was quiet and swift: a pot of strong tea, thick toast, and a note already waiting on the hall table. It bore Kent's brisk handwriting, summoning Mildred back to Brooklands for an urgent demonstration at Mr Pym's insistence. There was to be a practical test, open to all, under Hartley's strict supervision, to address festering doubts about safety, allegations, and that wretched coil.

By half-past nine, Mildred and Bea had returned and were crossing freshly cut lawns toward the pit bays. The freshness of overnight rain lent the world a clarity missing from the previous day; puddles stippled the approach road and cleaned the untidy footprints of suspicion, though not its residue. Journalists, committee women, and mechanics gathered anew, drawn by the promise of proof.

Pym, pale and close-shaven, was already arranging his demonstration stand outside a vacant pit, while Ada Finch unpacked handouts in nervous batches and Hartley stared at his twin watches as if their accuracy might keep events from sliding into chaos. Inspector Kent, appearing even more dapper after a few hours' sleep in the assistant steward's quarters, oversaw the assembly with a kind of watchdog patience.

"Not much rest for the righteous?" Bea yawned, sidling up beside Mildred as they reached the crowd.

"Or the curious," Mildred murmured. "Let's see if daylight brings honesty, or merely more polished lies."

Hartley brought the gathering to order with a double rap of his knuckles. "Mr Pym wishes to demonstrate the strength and integrity of his product after recent… unfounded whispers. All may witness and record the process. Our purpose is illumination, not scapegoating."

Pym gave a stiff nod and began. "Brooklands demands the highest standards. Today, we test a production batch in view of the club and the police." His voice was clear but strained.

"All cables here are marked and tagged as they are in regular issue."

He fitted a sample in his tensile testing rig. Mechanics pressed in, sceptical but attentive. The cable withstood 400 pounds with only a slight flex; when he applied further weight, it snapped but at a point far above what any racing condition would inflict.

Pym explained, "That's a controlled failure; clean break, exactly as designed. No fraying, no inclusion, no corrosion." He displayed the ends. Hartley checked them, consulted a chart, nodded satisfaction. The process repeated twice more; each time, the cable performed as claimed, the crowd's interest piqued but their suspicions not entirely cooled.

Then came a twist. A mechanic, Crib Davies, usually reliable, stepped forward with a battered coil he insisted had appeared in the scrap bin. Its tag, written in unsteady hand, read: "Bad —test only—Not for use."

Hartley peered at the label. "Not mine, nor Stringer's, nor Miss Finch's traditional hand." He eyed Pym. "Care to inspect it?"

Pym's face radiated frustration. "Certainly not one I've issued. Someone's playing games."

They tested this "bad" coil: it failed, snapping well below the expected threshold. A ripple of mutters coursed through the onlookers.

"Sabotage or plant?" Kent asked aloud, not so much for an answer as a warning.

Pym's expression was bleak. "An enemy's little show, I dare say. Not mine."

As the demonstration concluded, Hartley excused himself and made for his office in the Clubhouse. Mildred, reading the weather of his countenance, nodded to Bea. "Let's see if he's rattled by more than loose coils."

In the office, Hartley leafed through his correspondence drawer. To his surprise, a brown envelope, embossed with Pym's own winning monogram, slid into view. Not sealed, but loosely closed, as if recently disturbed.

With a frown, Hartley opened it. A wad of pound notes, and a slip inscribed, almost desperately, FOR COOPERATION— usher the demonstration to a fair conclusion. He glared up at Mildred and Kent, who'd just entered.

"Someone wants me to quash doubts outside procedure. I know nothing of this, I assure you."

Inspector Kent snapped on gloves and examined the sheet. Mildred leaned in, eyes narrowing on the envelope's telltale rip and its curious, rushed opening, torn from the "flap" side, not the seal one would present if truly seeking discretion.

"Have you the habit of keeping Mr Pym's stationery, Mr Hartley?" Mildred asked, tone careful.

Hartley drew himself up. "Certainly not. All communications come through proper channels, ask Miss Finch. She manages club correspondence single-handedly."

Kent's features remained tight. "Pym, would you care to comment?"

Pym strode in, summoned by Ada. His shock upon seeing the note turned to outrage. "This is not mine! My envelopes are locked. Only Miss Finch and I hold keys and one went missing a week ago. Anyone could have had access."

Ada, hovering in the doorway, nodded. "It's true. I lost the spare at tea last Friday. I told Mr Pym. I've searched everywhere; Maudie Knowles said she saw it in the side corridor, but it vanished before she could pick it up."

Mildred examined the note once more. The writing was heavy, unfamiliar, and, she suspected, deliberately shakier than proper. "Whoever handled this wanted it found, and fast. The torn seal is almost a signature for haste, or stagecraft."

Hartley, jaw set, squared his shoulders. "Inspector, please make this public. If someone wishes to smear my integrity, let them do so in daylight."

Out on the terrace, word of the bribe had already trickled out. Brooks peered over his notes. "A bribe so clumsy, and after such a public demonstration! Scandal sells, but this gives melodrama a bad name."

Rae, by the stands, kept her arms folded. "Anyone with access to the staff rooms could have filched the envelope and penned a scrawl."

Pym, pale and sweating, turned to Mildred. "I haven't offered a bribe, Lady Ramsay. I have rivals, and more than a few. All of them benefit if my credibility suffers, especially after Captain Mallory's demise."

She met Kent's eye. "This episode is not the work of a desperate man. A show bribe this crude, meant to be discovered, amounts to blackmail by rumour. It guarantees headlines and friction, not conclusions."

Hartley locked his drawer, handed the note and envelope to Kent, and called the mechanics to affirm his own process.

As the demonstration bled into another round of speculation, the sun skidded behind the Clubhouse roofs. Ada Finch retreated to the shade to stifle tears. Kent stood centre-ring, promising all evidence would "go straight to headquarters—no conclusions until forensics return."

Mildred found shade on the Club balcony beside Bea. "Some villain's delight," she murmured, "turning Brooklands into a parlour game for malice. Yet their skill is all in the staging. No proper forger would rip an envelope flap."

Bea passed her a handkerchief dampened with lavender. "All's theatre until the curtain falls, Millie. But the star performer may yet stumble."

Mildred watched Pym, hunched, gesturing helplessly to Kent. Ivy circled, ever protective of her committee's narrative. Brooks hunched over his next column. And Rae, almost alone among the racing crowd, seemed to have discounted the club's public theatre altogether, the look in her eyes confirming that the true hazards wore neither driving goggles nor pressed lapels.

One night, one day, and now a public spectacle engineered for something other than clarity. Even with a little more rest and sunlight, the plot had only thickened. Mildred suspected tomorrow would mean another summons, another round of performance and, she hoped, another inch of truth.

For if the saboteur's hand was so eager to direct attention that he'd risk a daylight bribe, perhaps desperation was finally setting in. And desperation, as Mildred well knew, always left fingerprints, especially when entangled in the mystery of the final lap at Brooklands, a place already steeped in graphite, shadows, and suspicion.

14

The safety demonstration's drama was still rippling across Brooklands when, late that afternoon, Mildred found herself in the quieter, high-ceilinged drawing room adjoining the Clubhouse. Here, the echoes of public bribes and brittle applause faded to a gentle hush; only the faint clink of porcelain and the muted exchange of confidences disturbed the room. In this rare oasis, where the air was perfumed by over-brewed Assam and traces of lavender polish, Mildred settled into a wide bay window seat with a welcome sigh.

Kent slipped in a moment later, presence as upright as ever but features worn. He looked, she thought, like a man who had spent the night on both a sofa and the horns of a dilemma. He poured himself tea and, with a nod to formality, accepted a bun from a tiered stand.

"Lady Ramsay," he greeted, resting his cup. "Do you always take your investigations with currants and cinnamon?"

"Always," Mildred replied lightly. "An army, they say, marches on its stomach. The same is true of reason; it cannot operate on nerves alone."

They sat for a moment, content in silence. The commotion from the safety demonstration thinned to distant voices. Mildred noted how Kent's hands, usually so steady, hovered now with a certain tension around his teaspoon.

"You could have used whisky," she offered, with gentle dry humour.

Kent's lips twitched, but he didn't smile. "I'd rather keep my wits, Lady Ramsay. I find they are in rather short supply on this case." He sipped. "We are under pressure to close the matter. The Brooklands board would like things... wrapped. Their notion of dignity, I expect."

Mildred watched him quietly, letting the braid of the moment settle. "Pressure from above, pressure all around. And then the innuendo—the envelope, the planted coil. Whoever lays these false trails relies on the hurry to do their work."

Kent set down his cup with a little more force than intended. "Do you know what I find most intolerable? Not the lies, not even the improvisations. Rather, it's the performances. Pym's outrage at the bribe, Ivy's careful sorrow, Brooks's theatrics for the press tent. Even the mechanics have started acting for an audience."

Mildred smiled, but her eyes were troubled. "No one ever puts on an act without hoping for applause. Or at the very least, distraction. People lie to hide big things, but they almost always start with the little ones, hoping to sneak the larger fiction through on habit."

Kent gave her a searching look. "You think our killer, our saboteur, built a stage first, then directed his actors?"

"I do." Mildred spoke quietly, weighing her words. "There's a pattern to the misdirection. The bribe, so clumsily planted, with its torn seal visible to anyone. The coil, so poorly tagged, destined to be found and discussed. It's all staged with the air of someone who wants us to look for scandal, not skill."

Kent nodded, rubbing his chin. "The show is meant to hurry us to an easy culprit. But we have too many loose threads for a simple knot. The typewritten threat, the rumour about Rae's midnight laps, Alf's old debt, Ivy's financial tangles with Pym, and now this, envelope planted for all to see. Each points a finger, but never quite closes the circle."

Mildred had poured a second cup without noticing. She drank. "People who lie in small ways, small switches, modest forgeries, do so out of nervous habit. But whoever cut that brake cable worked with method, not panic. That was the act of a craftsman, not a coward."

Kent's voice was low. "And one who knows the timetable down to the minute. I had a word with Dr Marsh this morning, when you were with Mrs Thwaite. Her estimate of time of death is exact. Mallory was killed within the three-minute window you traced with Hartley."

He produced a notebook and laid it between them. "Here, the time from the moment Alf last checked the car, to when Mallory mounted, is three minutes, never quite four. If the brake cable was scored, tampered with, or trick-wired, it had to be done by someone who could move in and out unseen, and who knew the exact moment to act."

"So," Mildred mused, "not a rank amateur. It narrows things, at least in theory."

He nodded. "And it heightens the nerve required. Tampering was done in public, while the paddock bustled. It's less a crime of passion than of calculation. I begin to think our saboteur, our murderer, must be someone who rehearses, not improvises."

They fell silent, both lost in thought. The crackle of coal on the grate punctuated an interval of reflection. Outside, the sky was receding into lead-grey, the circuit drawn sharp as a blueprint.

Mildred set aside her cup. "So, we have three types before us, Inspector: the improviser, the rehearsed, and the actor."

Kent's mouth curved. "You'd like to assign roles, I see?"

"Let's consider them," Mildred replied, enjoying the exercise. "Brooks is an improviser. Always quick with his tongue and camera, never quite where expected, but rarely preparing too far in advance. He's used to shaping a story post hoc. Ivy is the master of staged drama. Her grief, her charity, her concern, it's all played for the committee, and she never misses an entrance. But method? I doubt that's her strength."

Kent agreed softly. "Pym rehearses every demonstration, every sentence. Even his denials are polished. Ada, too, she keeps records to the point of obsession."

Mildred continued, "Alf and the mechanics are creatures of habit. Routine protects them, but it also makes them vulnerable if the routine is breached. Rae... Rae's precision is the spirit of racing itself, but she is less an actor than a technician. She does not like distractions, only what is needful."

"And you?" Kent's voice was playful.

"I," Mildred answered, "prefer to watch and wait. An audience rather than an actor."

Kent chuckled. "Yet you are here at every stage, Lady Ramsay."

Just then, Mrs Thwaite appeared with a jug. "More tea, dear lady?" she asked, a bright glimmer in her eyes, as if she suspected herself part of a far larger drama. "You and the

Inspector have the look of two actors about to rewrite the script."

"Something like that," Mildred replied, her voice gentle as she refilled her cup. "Every investigation is a play. One must observe which gestures are nervous tics and which are cunning cues."

Mrs Thwaite leaned in, lowering her voice. "If you care for my opinion, I'd say Mr Pym rehearses until he makes mistakes. Miss Finch is anxious but truthful, and Brooks, well, that one loves a crowd, but he sees more than he says."

As she left, Kent caught Mildred's eye. "There's wisdom. She sees the surface, but not the knots beneath."

"Precisely," said Mildred, "which is why we must look not just at rehearsals, but at the little spontaneous moments. The saboteur must have staged their scene, but they may have told the truth in a careless aside."

Kent closed his notebook. "So, tomorrow we test habits. We ask about routines and see who trips. We encourage improvisation, and see who prefers the comfort of a prepared speech. We ask each for their memories of the morning, unscripted, if possible."

Mildred nodded. "And we watch for those who resist even the simplest cues. Those who would rather control every entrance and exit than admit to a single moment of disorder. Because it's control, not chaos, that drove the murder."

She tucked her notebook away. "We're close, Inspector Kent. We're closer than we know."

He smiled, more freely now, some of the tiredness dispelled. "Tea is restorative," he said quietly. "But truth is more so. Let's finish the day as we began. Method for me, motive for you. Together, we may yet undo the script written in haste."

As dusk pressed close upon the glass, Mildred let herself imagine the knots loosening, the actors making their final curtain call. She pictured the saboteur rehearsing, alone, somewhere on the storied circuit, never thinking that someone had already marked the true measure of their act.

Tomorrow, then: a test of method and motive together. And beneath it all, Mildred's clear promise to herself, if the liar was hiding among small deceits, she would find that space, lay bare the fiction, and write the ending anew.

15

Evening had drawn a hush over Brooklands, but in the aftermath of tea with Inspector Kent, Mildred's mind remained animated; a wheel, turning and ticking over old words, new suspicions. Their agreement to probe routine, habit, and the tiny improvisations that betray a performance still echoed in her thoughts as she left the Clubhouse and strode across the cooling gravel towards the paddock workshops.

The air was sharper, cut through with the ghost of burnt fuel and the green bite of mown grass. Mechanics loitered by the garages in the lull before supper, voices low. Overhead, the tower's banner drooped in the breathless dusk. Alf Keating was keeping company, sulky and steadfast, with a cup of tea and a hunk of bread at his bay's threshold. His hands, usually decisive, now worried the rim of his mug, picking at flecks of oil that clung despite his recent efforts with soap.

Mildred approached, steps brisk and hopeful. She had seen the look in Alf's eyes before; defence shading toward defeat. In the corners of those eyes, lines had etched themselves deeper since the crash.

"Mr Keating," she greeted, her voice soft enough for the hour, "will you grant me a little indulgence?"

He started, mustering a half-hearted scowl, but there was no heat in it. "Lady Ramsay, this isn't a great moment for favours."

She gave him a gentle, conspiratorial smile. "I can't promise to leave you in peace, but perhaps I might leave your conscience a little clearer. I'd like to see that infamous spares drawer everyone mutters about. For my own curiosity, no Inspector in tow."

He eyed her, then nodded with grudging respect. "Don't much like anyone poking in there. Some things… best left alone. Still, you're not the sort to turn a spanner just for the thrill."

He led her to the workbench bolted along the garage wall, where a battered black drawer, heavy with years and memory, waited beneath a clutch of spare parts. Alf fished out a key from his breast pocket and unlocked it. There was a faint click, oddly loud in the settling evening.

The drawer slid open with a reluctant groan, revealing its trove: brake linings, cotter pins, a faded box of electrical fuses, tubes of grease, and, laid on top, wrapped in waxed cloth, a brake cable.

Alf handled the bundle with the care usually reserved for something fragile or dangerous. He unwrapped it and laid it on the bench. Immediately, Mildred could see what set this piece apart: an old cut, nearly halfway through the sheath, now dulled by age and a rim of corrosion. A slanting tag, tied with waxed thread, fluttered from one end: "Bad—keep for demonstration."

She ran a finger just above the cut, careful not to touch the sharp maw in the metal. It looked purposeful, not the work of fatigue or accident. In different hands, or interpreted for a different reason, it might be proof of the very sort of malice she was hunting.

She examined the tag, noting the upward slant of the writing, the clear, practical hand, faintly familiar. "That's a tidy label, Mr Keating. Not yours?"

He shook his head, glancing over his shoulder. "I can't spell without looking twice, Lady Ramsay. Rae writes 'em, neat as clockface. She insists, says every apprentice needs to see what not to do before they try it for real."

A beat, a little defensiveness in his voice. "She'd never let one of these out on a real car. No more would I."

Mildred nodded. "But it does raise a point. If someone wanted to confuse matters, or plant evidence, the easiest way would be to swap a training piece for the real thing in a rush, in the crowd. Or to make a tag look official."

Alf frowned. "Only Rae and me ever open this drawer. I lock it every night. Key's on me, chained so I can't lose it."

"Could you have been distracted?" Mildred asked. "Or worse, could someone have got close when your back was turned?"

He scowled at the suggestion, but after a moment, perhaps recalling the uproar and confusion in the paddock before Mallory's crash, his expression shifted to one of worry. "Maybe. It was chaos that morning. I left for five, ten minutes… ran to the stores for a fuse. Peter Finch, who was sorting gaskets then, could've walked past."

As Alf recounted this, Bea slipped through the sliding doors behind them, slippers quiet on the concrete. She carried a plate of ill-advisedly assembled sandwiches, which she distributed between herself and Mildred.

"Food for courage!" she murmured. "It's like being back at the front, isn't it, pivoting off secrets on bread and tea."

She peered into the open drawer with frank curiosity. "Oh, that's a neat little tag, Rae's hand?" She ran her thumb over the paper, then wrinkled her brow. "Look at this... the ink's fresh at the loop, but faded otherwise. Someone used a new pen, or maybe rewrote the knot. See how it ghosts along the edge?"

Mildred studied the label afresh. Bea had a gift for noticing the small moods of objects: the tag's string had indeed a faint blue glow at the knot, while the older text bore the brown tint of a much-used nib. "Very good, Bea. Fresh ink where the thread doubles, but the body's been handled often. Someone retied this, and not so long ago by the look of it."

Alf's worry deepened. "That's not right. Why would anyone fiddle with a tag if not to—"

"To swap it perhaps?" Mildred finished gently. "Or simply to make an honest piece appear suspect."

He ran a hand through his short hair. "Rae labels all our bad cables. Could someone mean to make it look like she planted a dud?"

"We mustn't jump," Mildred cautioned, "but Rae's scrupulousness might have made her a target. If someone mocked up an old cut, retagged it, and left it handy... well, that could be a double trap."

Bea, munching her sandwich, mused aloud. "Or, it could be red ink in a blue bottle, as Mrs Thwaite would say. Who else has the patience and the hand to forge Rae's tags? Pym's Ada writes very fine labels, I've seen her at it. Hartley's a lefty, but not this shape."

THE MYSTERY OF THE FINAL LAP

Alf interjected, "Peter Finch worked with Rae last. Maybe he watched her doing the tags. That kid's eager, but apt to copy whatever works. Doesn't always see what's underneath."

The thought sobered the trio. The web was intricate: honest demonstration parts turned weapons of suspicion, diligence morphed, by one twist of string or pen, into implied sabotage.

Mildred tested another hypothesis. "Could the real saboteur have known Rae's habits, counted on her to label her bad cable and tuck it here? Then, in the bustle, slipped away the original and replaced it with the one used on Mallory's car?"

Alf shook his head. "Mallory's car didn't have any of our marked bits. He liked his own spares—'from home', he called them. But if the right tag was stolen, it would be enough to throw doubt. The kind of plan that takes weeks, and knowing folk's ways."

Bea wrinkled her nose. "That much cleverness for so petty a gain?"

But Mildred was thinking, turning the tag, the ink, the old cut, about habit and intent. "For some, the small, plausible lie is the only one worth telling. One swaps the label, not the cable. One sprinkles a bit of graphite where oil should be, knowing it vanishes in the crowd."

A faint whirring from outside. Brooks wandered past, trailing a notebook, whistling a tune whose brightness belied its origin. He gave the trio a genial wave. "Cabinet of curiosities in here!" he called. "Shall I fetch my camera for posterity or do we keep this one for the club's secrets?"

"Best keep it off the record for now, Mr Brooks," Mildred returned, raising an eyebrow.

He grinned, ducked his head, took a moment to glance, a

little too quickly, she thought, at the contents of the drawer, and moved on.

As silence returned, Bea whispered. "So who, Mildred, inherits this muddle?"

Mildred drew a steadying breath. "Someone who moves with us, knows our arrangements, and can improvise within the well-worn rehearsals of the club. A person who rehearses misdirection, but has a habit for real things, spares, tags, and the routine mechanics of trust."

They replaced the cable carefully, relocking the drawer. Alf watched with a wary pride. "First left the tag years ago for the juniors. Never thought it'd end up a subject for a tribunal."

Mildred clapped his shoulder. "You kept faith. Whether it's diligence or design, you gave us a point of clarity. That matters now, more than ever."

As they left the garage, the polish of doubt glimmered along the spares drawer's seam. Mildred guided Bea back toward the Clubhouse, glancing at the emptied paddock. Talks from tea carried in snatches on the evening breeze: mechanics griping, the press rewriting headlines, Ivy's committee cycling through the day's script.

Bea, always the stronger for her optimism, squeezed Mildred's hand. "We're closer, aren't we? Closer than any lie to the truth."

Mildred nodded, feeling it. The small, tidy clues had started to cry out their purpose; habits might yet be the saboteur's undoing. As the shadows lengthened and the club prepared for another restless night, she was certain the answer was not somewhere new, but somewhere familiar. In ink, new and old. In the trust of honest hands. In the little betrayals of routine.

She looked back just once at the old drawer, now safely shut, and resolved that if the saboteur trusted in old habits and small lies, it was up to her to catch the hand, gentle or not, that had set them in motion.

16

The evening was drawing in again, a sudden dusk sparked by low cloud and the slow extinguishing of the day. In the aftermath of their search of Alf's spares drawer, Mildred and Bea had returned to the Clubhouse for supper, a subdued affair dominated by rain hissing against the tall windows and the faint, endless rhythm of speculation among those still lingering at Brooklands.

Yet satisfaction eluded Mildred. Doubt had found its roost in her mind, and as she mulled the fresh-inked tag in Alf's drawer, a sign of either dodged guilt or devious interference, she was struck again by how much at Brooklands was both meticulously routine and dangerously exposed. Trust here could be as easily rewound as a cable's tag.

It was after the second serving of Mrs Thwaite's apple sponge, during which Kent had retreated to check the progress of Dr Marsh's forensic analysis, that Hartley approached them at their chosen table by the window.

He was less brisk than usual, mouth set in a line of near-embarrassment above his famous pocket watches. "Lady Ramsay, Lady Mortimer," he said, voice pitched low, "I may have been hasty in restricting access to certain personal effects. The Inspector has asked me to permit you to search Captain Mallory's locker, should you wish it. It's down by the north end, second row, left-side string. Alf has already given permission. After all, if there's a clue to be found, I'd trust you to find it."

Mildred, always tactful, nodded in gratitude. "Thank you, Mr Hartley. We're grateful for the trust. Shall we, Bea?"

The rain had eased to a thick drizzle as they left the Clubhouse. The cupped glow of the yard's few lamps rolled their shadows out and away, lending the walk to the locker room a sense of minor adventure. There, under the corrugated roof and the smell of rubber and oil, the rows of lockers lay in drowsy, metallic wait.

Hartley's keys, so numerous they clashed together like the bellman's at the Midland Grand, winnowed the locks until the proper one snapped home. "Take your time," he intoned, and withdrew discreetly.

Inside the spare, clean locker, everything was as neat as a naval kit inspection. Mallory had been a military man to the end: one spare pair of goggles, a copy of Blackwood's Magazine, rolled gloves, a flask as yet untouched. Bea's fingers hovered at the shallow shelf. "Nothing amiss, nothing surprising. He travelled light for a man with so heavy a reputation."

Mildred lifted down a small satchel tucked into the right-hand corner. Inside was a chamois pouch containing the expected odds and ends: a roll of coins, a matchbook, and, folded square, a battered leather pocketbook.

She opened the pocketbook with reverence, thinking of all the unlikely objects upon which answers sometimes precariously perched. A waft of old paper and pipe tobacco escaped. The first leaf was a neat note, written in an upright, slightly old-fashioned hand:

"Alf—take this and settle the matter with Hobson. Repay me if you like, or don't—what matters is that nonsense doesn't follow you from the track. R."

Below the note was tucked a receipt: an IOU, marked paid, from the bookmaker in town. The sum was not insubstantial, but nothing to a man of Mallory's means. Bea drew a sharp breath. "So that's the end of that speculation. Alf's debts were done with. Mallory saw him clear."

"It reads as much like an act of friendship as an act of caution," Mildred said quietly. "He did not want a good man ruined or tempted."

A slim sheaf of correspondence made up the rest of the pocketbook. Mildred thumbed through messages from various corners of Mallory's life, a letter from a sister, a Post Office receipt, a racing calendar with a ticking pencil. Then, on a separate sheet of thick, war-era stationery, she found what looked initially like a draft. The writing was his again; broader but tense:

"Regretfully decline endorsement. I do not find the new Modern Eng. Solutions cable a material improvement, nor do I wish my name lent to experiments. I value reliability above novelty, and my public support shall not be bought."

He had signed only his initials, but there it was: clear as a racing stripe, for Pym, a firm and final 'no'.

Bea whistled gently. "Express and unequivocal, as the lawyers say."

There was another slip, pencilled at the margin of a committee schedule:

"Meeting: Ivy C. — speech on safety/profiteering? Query future invitations? Must speak plainly."

Mildred and Bea exchanged glances. "So he planned not only to withhold endorsement from Pym, but also to speak about club profiteering, likely the sponsorships and oddments of Lady Carrington's committee," Mildred observed.

A heavier truth slipped into the space between them: here, neatly pressed between the everyday tokens of Mallory's life, lay the roots of so many tensions; the notes struck a clear chord with everything the past week at Brooklands had exposed.

They worked in silence for a while, searching for anything overlooked: an address tucked between two receipts, a circuit diagram of the banking, dog-eared by much handling, but nothing more of note. Satisfied, Mildred replaced the effects—except for the bequest and the refusal, which she tucked carefully into her handbag, intending to show Kent.

Locking the door behind them, they found Hartley waiting with his usual propriety just at the edge of the awning, umbrella folded and raindrops glimmering on his coat. He seemed less the brisk steward and more the man momentarily saddened by the unravelling of a world he'd tended so well.

"Captain Mallory kept discipline in all things," he said, voice soft in the damp air. "He would have hated the mess, but he'd have wanted the truth even more. I hope you found what you needed, Lady Ramsay."

"We did, Mr Hartley," Mildred replied.

On their way back to the Clubhouse, wrapped against the mist, Bea pondered aloud. "So much comes down to him, doesn't it, Millie? He refused Pym, so Pym's pride and reputation were injured. He would have spoken on safety and profiteering, so Ivy and her committee stood to be embarrassed, maybe even lose standing. Alf's future, so bound to Mallory's generosity, yet twisted by others into motive for murder. And then there's Rae, so often in his shadow. She must have seen his stance as both a barrier and a challenge."

"Motives as massed as rain clouds," Mildred murmured. "But what of the method? We know what people hoped for, feared, or resented. The trick is who turned motive into sabotage, and who may have later sought to frame or confuse matters further."

They passed the press tent, where a bustle signalled another cocktail of deadlines and gossip. Bea, recovering her brightness, added, "You realise there's an intense irony, darling, so many people with secrets locked tight, only for us to find answers in the one place everyone believed was closed to outsiders."

Mildred smiled. "There is a certain narrative pleasure in that, isn't there? Still, much as our friend Brooks would enjoy the symmetry, it's the truth, not the shape of the story, that matters most. We now know for certain Alf's supposed motive was old history. As for the rest, the day grows short on lies and long on clarity."

Inside, they found Kent warming his hands before the fire in the smaller lounge. He seemed a little lighter, perhaps in anticipation of Dr Marsh's promised report, but did not lose his gravity on receiving the pocketbook and its contents. He nodded as Mildred quietly summarised their findings.

"I expected as much of Mallory," he said. "His types are rare. I'd trust him to command a field, or a pit. Poor Alf, cleared of one dark cloud, but still under the weather of suspicion thanks to a world too fond of the obvious answer."

He read the note declining Pym's cable and the pencilled schedule. "He was not a subtle adversary. He said what he thought, and did as he pleased. That type can make more enemies in a year of integrity than most do in a life of compromise."

"Except," Mildred added, "that someone has gone to such lengths to embroil others: Alf with his debt, Rae with her rivalry, Pym with his product, Ivy with her committee's reputation. All justified by Mallory's refusal to play the expected part. There's a web here, Kent, a clever one. Woven to exploit the very routines and habits we probed this morning."

Kent nodded thoughtfully. "We have strong threads now, enough, perhaps, to begin unpicking. The forensics may tell us which cable was tampered with, but the reason why lies in this pocketbook: principle, resistance to flattery, and an inconvenient inclination for honesty."

As the evening deepened, Mildred felt a shift; a gathering of purpose, an unspoken agreement that the final acts were upon them. The drama at Brooklands was no longer about speculation, performance, or rumour, but about the patient collection and weighing of real evidence. The rhythms of motive were clear; now, only the hand, skilled and familiar, that wrought the fatal act remained to be revealed.

Bea, watching the fire, added with quiet force, "Sometimes, it's the one who spends most time in the wings who manages the most clever business onstage."

Mildred let the thought linger. They were closing in; the story was nearly told. All that remained was to test each habit, scrutinise the telltale improvisations, and wait for the murderer, so careful with method, so expert in the theatre of misdirection, to drop one final, fatal cue.

17

The dawn that broke over Brooklands was muted, shrouded by low-lying cloud and a damp chill that seeped through gloves and overcoats. It was the sort of weather that made all but the determined remain abed, and it left the circuit feeling secretive, a hush disturbed only by the distant clink of wrenches and the first tentative testing of engines.

Lady Mildred Ramsay, however, had never cared much for comfort when answers were close at hand. After her discoveries with Bea in Mallory's locker, she'd slept uneasily, her mind replaying the significance of each page. When she made her way across the bracing paddock, Bea in tow, cheeks ruddy from the cold and adventure, she found Rae St John already at work outside the garages, sleeves rolled, cap askew, and a glint of fatigue in her eyes that spoke of little sleep and much rumination.

"Perfect timing, Lady Ramsay," Rae called, not looking up from her adjustments. "I've a demonstration to set, and your Ladyship's friend has volunteered as my unfortunate test subject."

Mildred raised an eyebrow, suspicion and amusement mingling. "Have you, Bea?"

Bea grinned, patting the thick scarf at her throat. "I saw the state of that motor and thought, 'if it kills me, they'll at least write a better column than anything Brooks can churn out.' Besides, Mrs Thwaite says spin before breakfast sharpens the wits."

The car in question was a battered Humber saloon, famous among the paddock as "the indestructible." Rae gestured for Bea to climb into the passenger seat, while Mildred positioned herself near the bonnet, eyes keen on the interplay of hands and hardware.

Inside, the controls bore the wear of years: the faded bakelite lever, the hard-won smoothness of a brake pedal polished by thousands of cautious feet. Rae called instructions over her shoulder, voice clipped and steady.

"Just a single lap down the access road, then a slow swing round the banking's southern edge. Nothing faster than twenty, Lady Beatrice. This car's cleverer than all of us, but she's stubborn when cold."

Bea, eyes wide and hands careful, nodded. Rae fired the ignition with a practiced flick, engine catching, unevenly at first, then settling to a lazy thrum.

As they moved off, Mildred tracked every detail: the way Rae's left hand rested near the gear lever, the way her right foot hovered over pedals in readiness to intervene, and Bea's delighted gasp as they rolled forward. Midway down the straight, with Rae guiding and Bea steering, the car lurched—sudden, sharp, as if tripped by an invisible hand beneath the dashboard.

"Dash it all!" Bea's voice was brittle with surprise.

THE MYSTERY OF THE FINAL LAP

The saloon swerved erratically, slowed by its own momentum, before Rae stamped in to steady the motor and guide them to a halt. She leaned over, examining the footwell.

"What on earth—?" Bea exclaimed, pulling her left heel free from its surprising entanglement.

Rae extracted a slender piece of wire, perhaps three inches, thin as a hairpin, from under the brake lever. She held it aloft, eyes narrowed.

"There's your problem. Lady Beatrice has a dainty foot, but if the heel catches—" she demonstrated, hooking the wire where the pedal curved—"the effect's the same as if someone had inserted a deliberate obstruction or false linkage."

Mildred examined the wire carefully. "This doesn't look ordinary. What exactly is it?"

Rae nodded. 'Throttle linkage wire. Thin enough for temporary repairs, but in the wrong hands, it could easily cause a dangerous malfunction."

Bea massaged her ankle, more amused than shaken. "I assure you, I had no sinister intention, Mildred. But that jump, goodness, it was as though the car wanted a mind of its own."

Rae handed the wire to Mildred for closer examination. "See here, the ends are sharp, not weathered. Pulled from a spool this morning, I'd wager."

Mildred ran her finger thoughtfully beneath the pedal, reconstructing the event. "A trick as old as the first racing contest: insert an unexpected wire, a nut, anything to catch at the crucial moment. If the car lurches, who blames sabotage? It always appears as driver error or, if you're unlucky, careless maintenance."

Rae's expression hardened. "It's how they taught us in the Ambulance Corps. Always trace mechanical failure to its smallest cause, a pebble in the shoe, a missing cotter pin, or, as here, a cunning bit of wire. In the right hands, it's repair; in the wrong, mischief."

Mildred pocketed the wire, her pulse now sharper from suspicion than the brisk morning breeze. "Could someone have set this before you came, Miss St John?"

Rae shook her head. "Only myself and Peter Finch have handled this car since I checked it yesterday. Then again, anyone with a little nerve and a good sense of where to stand while eyes are distracted, could do as much."

They walked the short distance around the bays while Bea, now fully alert and unflustered, recounted her experience for a gathering knot of curious mechanics and two young drivers with club badges. Brooks wandered up, notepad ready, sniffing opportunity in the air.

"Did our Lady Beatrice nearly best your record?" he quipped, with his usual mixture of mischief and admiration.

"She missed the shrubbery by a hair," Rae announced deliberately, "but the lesson's this: always check the controls for anything out of place before trusting a machine, especially at Brooklands."

One of the drivers, a bright-eyed youth named Davis, mused aloud. "We use wires like that for all sorts. Connecting kill-switches, patching relays…"

Mildred turned to him, interested. "And could such a wire, if set just so, simulate a failure in a brake or throttle?"

"Easily," Davis replied, proud to be consulted. "You run it under or alongside a pedal, catch it on the return. Done right, the delay's just enough, or too much, depending. If someone wanted to make it look like your fault, it'd fool even a race steward."

Brooks scribbled furiously. "No shortage of suspects with access, then."

Rae snapped the bonnet shut, surveying her own handiwork ruefully. "No shortage of those who know too much, and care too little."

As the trio regrouped at the bay, Mildred extracted the wire and held it up in the rising light. "This, I think, is both key and cipher. Who slipped it in, did so knowing not only about the car, but about timing and opportunity. It's not a thing one does on a whim. It needs coolness, a rehearsed action, disguised by apparent chaos."

Bea, washing oil from her gloves with a rag, offered, "In the right hands, such a wire is a blessing; in the wrong, it's evidence, if only we can connect it to the right moment and the right suspect."

Mildred's gaze was faraway as she reviewed what they'd learned. The planted wire offered a practical explanation for how even a careful driver could be made to err, and how the saboteur might have created or mimicked, just such a lurch in Mallory's fatal lap. She could picture it: a brief distraction, a retreating figure vanishing into the crowd, a glove with traces of graphite and wire-shards. All the old routines at Brooklands, married to a moment's cruel improvisation.

As they left the Humber and returned to the paddock for a hard-earned breakfast, Mildred kept the wire close, intent on matching it to the materials in Alf's spares and the ones Pym's firm used for demonstrations. Only a handful of people could claim knowledge of both, yet nearly anyone, it seemed, could have had opportunity.

Over mugs of tea and slabs of Mrs Thwaite's fruit cake, the day settled into its steady, anxious tempo. The circuit hummed with anticipation: not only for the looming inquest, but for Kent's promised round of fresh interviews and Dr Marsh's soon-to-arrive forensic report. Brooks circulated, half-joking, half-serious, about whether saboteurs preferred whisky or tea as their morning tipple.

When Kent appeared, notebook in hand and eyes sharp, Mildred was ready. She produced the length of wire, recounted Bea's near-mishap, Rae's confirmation of the wire's origin, and Davis's insight.

Kent examined it thoughtfully. "So small a thing, so dangerous a consequence. What makes sabotage so insidious is precisely this: plausibility masquerading as bad luck."

"Or as carelessness," Mildred added. "Placed just so, it implicates whoever the crowd already suspects. It's a magician's trick, misdirection by drama, and concealment by routine."

Kent's brow furrowed. "Which fits our larger pattern: the amateurish bribe, the swapped tag, the staged demonstrations. But the murderer is no amateur at heart. Only the staging is crude. The actions are precise, hidden in plain sight."

Bea, adjusting her scarf with dramatic flair, declared, "I've a new respect for cautious footwork and good gloves. And if I am called upon for another demonstration, Mildred, do see that the wire is properly accounted for."

Rae smirked. "That goes for you, too. I've got enough trouble keeping my own apprentices from sabotaging breakfast, let alone lap records."

Breakfast concluded, Mildred and Bea strolled toward the Clubhouse veranda. The sun had broken through at last, glancing off the famous banking and lighting up the involved faces below. For a moment, the circuit felt almost as it had in another, less troubled season, full of promise rather than peril.

THE MYSTERY OF THE FINAL LAP

As Mildred glanced at the gleaming curve of the track, her mind spun theory after theory. Today, she resolved, she would follow every spur. Wire, tag, graphite, cable, all might yet lead, through the ordinary habits of extraordinary people, to the central, concealed truth.

And if the saboteur made one last error, a careless wire, a misnamed label, a reckless word, Mildred was ready to see it for what it truly was: the overlooked thread that, finally, would unravel the tangle that threatened to choke all of Brooklands.

18

The lilt and clang of breakfast still echoed through the Clubhouse corridors as Mildred found her way to the medical office in the north wing; a new, faintly antiseptic addition to Brooklands, its windows thrown open to admit the reluctant autumn breeze. Dr Verity Marsh, starched but brisk, had established her domain among shelves of gauze and steel tins; on the desk, a promisingly thick file was already stacked with evidence.

It was here, having sent word for Mildred, Inspector Kent, and, discreetly, Alf Keating, that Dr Marsh meant to share her findings. The atmosphere in the little room was one of nerves just barely contained: Alf hovered by the door, hat in hand, while Kent stood straight at the desk, his face a careful mask. Mildred slipped onto a wooden chair near the window, grateful to see Dr Marsh, chin up, greeting each with unsentimental precision.

"Thank you for coming," Dr Marsh began with her usual clipped candour. "The forensic analysis is complete. I trust you'll forgive the details. I'm compelled to be thorough."

"We would expect nothing less," said Kent, eyes never leaving the papers.

Marsh nodded. "First, the critical matter, Captain Mallory's cause of death. My findings confirm the window you and Lady Ramsay established: traumatic impact occurred within minutes of his departure, as anticipated. What's more interesting is the state of the cable and the evidence from his gloves and clothing."

She flipped a page, finger tapping the margin. "On examination, Mallory's hands show no abrasions apart from two friction burns, both on the outer palm, the sort you find when a man fights to control a wheel experiencing sudden, unexpected resistance. Most telling: the burns correspond to a rapid, involuntary grasp, not the lingering hold you'd expect in a drawn-out loss of control."

Mildred, eyebrows raised, followed the implication. "So, he was trying to brake or recover at the last moment. Not struggling beforehand."

"Exactly," Marsh replied. "It wasn't a fire that finished it, nor even immediate collision. It was clearly catastrophic braking. Far too quick for the track conditions and not consistent with his reputation as a conservative driver."

She consulted another slip. "The cable taken from the car, as tested by Mr Pym and recorded by Mr Hartley, displays scoring that matches the pattern of an artificial cut—sharp, angled, and deep enough to prompt early failure under stress. Crucially, the residue at the site is graphite, not oil, which aligns with the observations Lady Ramsay and Inspector Kent made previously."

Kent leaned forward. "In other words, sabotage. Planned, not accidental."

"Without doubt." Marsh's voice was cool and instructive. "Had it been a matter of wear, we would see different marks—progressive stress, not an acute failing. Someone engineered this outcome."

Alf, silent until now, shifted awkwardly. "Excuse me, Doctor, but about my cuffs—"

Marsh smiled with the gentleness of experience. "Yes, Mr Keating. We analysed your cuffs for chemical traces. The white granules are battery acid, distinct from the acids found in modern brake fluid. They're consistent with the accumulator maintenance you logged that morning, as witnessed by at least two mechanics. No evidence links them to the brake cable tampering. You're not exonerated by magic, but by chemistry and good record-keeping."

Alf exhaled visibly, some of the stocky tension leaving his shoulders. But Marsh was not finished.

"There was, however, another faint trace detected—benzole, clinging to your coat, especially the sleeve. Not a damning sign in itself, but it suggests, as you told Inspector Kent, you handled the drums that morning. It's the sort of scent that lingers; the men from the stores confirmed you were among those to move the supplies before the first demonstration, correct?"

Alf nodded. "Yes, Doctor. First thing, helped Stringer shift them so the loaders could get to the new stock. That's all. Never touched any for Mallory's run, I swear."

"We believe you," Mildred said gently, thinking of how many hands touched a day's worth of tasks here. "But every tiny thing becomes significant in the wake of murder."

Marsh inclined her head, passing across the next set of notes. "And that brings me to Mallory's final moments. No bruising on the knuckles, no torn cuticles, and no embedded foreign matter. For a man who died gripping his wheel, he showed no defensive effort, no sign of a blow or struggle. The conclusion is inescapable, the sabotage occurred some time before he mounted the car. There is not even a hint that he had a clue until that fateful second, when his braking failed and the accident was inevitable."

For a moment, the weight of the room pressed in. Alf kept his gaze fixed on some private horizon. Kent tapped a pencil, brow furrowed in thought. Mildred studied the drawn faces, one by one marking the clearance of guilt, the narrowing field of the possible.

"I think," Kent said softly, "that removes any final credibility from the claim that Mallory's mistakes led to his end. Whoever tampered did so with cold forethought."

"Cold and clever," Marsh replied. "The friction burns are symmetrical. No broken nails. No grazes suggesting a struggle in the cockpit. Death was swift, and momentary; even tragic luck would have provided some warning. Mallory, by all accounts and every material fact at my disposal, was not at fault."

Alf's relief lingered, but was tinged with bitterness. "Still feels like I ought to have seen it, even if I didn't do it."

Mildred gave him a kind, searching look. "That's how decency endures, Mr Keating. But the facts are on your side now."

Dr Marsh gathered her files. "There's one more detail. The shoes. Mallory's left boot bore a thin, silvered scrape, recent, curved in a way suggestive of a wire or foreign body being dragged beneath the arch. The corresponding rubber on the pedal is slightly scored. I suspect, from the length and position, that something, a length of wire, perhaps, was temporarily installed, then released by force during the fatal lurch. The kind of thing that needs only a clever hand and a moment's distraction."

Kent glanced over at Mildred, eyes intent. "Like the trick wire you discovered with Miss St John?"

"Near identical in effect," Mildred said thoughtfully. "A trick any club mechanic might know or any journalist with the right expertise and nerve."

Marsh closed the file. "You now have a narrow window, an unequivocal means, and, I think, the clearest evidence of all: premeditation rather than impulse."

The interview drifted towards practicalities, statements for the inquest, the delivery of forensic samples to Scotland Yard, Kent's plans for one last sweep of the paddock. But the sense of purpose had shifted: now each piece was sharper, more irrefutable.

Afterwards, Mildred lingered as the others dispersed, staring down into the medical garden that Mrs Thwaite maintained with tenacious pride, herb and roses both, despite the petrol wind. She thought of Mallory's pocketbook: his bequest to Alf, his implacable letter to Pym, his desire for clean racing and honest speech. Here was a man whose enemies were many and whose integrity, in the right light, was as much a provocation as a shield.

She was joined by Bea, who had observed from the door. "How many times do you think people punish others for being righteous?"

"Always as many as can't bear to be found lacking," Mildred replied, voice soft. "In this place? Honour is both weapon and target."

Bea glanced at her hands; the pale blue ink of a letter she'd written to her mother earlier that morning still not quite washed away. "What now? There's motive and means, but so many hands near every clue."

"We focus on the hands, then," Mildred answered. "Graphite, lampblack, spare tags, and wire. Whoever handled those, and when. Not only the mechanics, but the press. And not only them, anyone who can move without attention at Brooklands is suspect."

She stepped back into the room, glancing one final time at the clinical paraphernalia, at Dr Marsh's steady hand and still-inked margin notes. "If we're to outwit the murderer," Mildred said quietly, "it's not enough to find means and motive. We must show habit; forged, borrowed, or betrayed."

Kent met her glance in the corridor, a silent understanding passing between them. Tomorrow would bring fresh interviews: old routines tested, new lies measured, every person's comfort with routine or performance called into account.

As Mildred walked away into the afternoon's gathering bustle, she realised Brooklands was a place defined by routine and that routine, so carefully kept for safety and sport, might be the very shield behind which murder hid. But it was also, she thought, a place where the smallest innovation, a wire, a tag, a cut, could be the undoing of the cleverest plan.

She could feel the circle tightening: Mallory had not erred, Alf was cleared, and sabotage had been coolly plotted in full sight of tradition. Brooklands was a stage for routine, but it would take just a little slip, one more overlooked gesture, one too-familiar action, for the murderer's mask to fall at last.

19

The morning after Dr Marsh's revelations, Brooklands stirred with a taut, restless energy, as if the great racing track itself sensed the net drawing tighter around a hidden killer. At breakfast, the Clubhouse dining room was a shifting landscape of wary glances and low-voiced speculation, with only the scent of sharp marmalade and strong black tea remaining reliably familiar.

Mildred found herself less interested in breakfast than most. She was up early to comb through the litter of records and personal effects Kent had corralled from the press tent, determined that today's little truths not slip into tomorrow's faulty recollections. Kent was occupied elsewhere, gently testing alibis and watching hands, so Mildred sought her own threads to untangle.

There, in the press's makeshift 'office'—actually an annex of the Club reading room—she discovered a sheaf of rough-typed pages. Lionel Brooks's typewriter stood to one side, the ribbon clattering yellower with each new act of journalistic industry. Brooks himself, out-charming Mrs Thwaite and the morning staff, was not there to defend his prose or his privacy.

Mildred took the liberty to riffle through the pile; nothing so vulgar as burglary, merely the curiosity of an unofficial archivist. Wedged among drafts and bun-crumbed sketches was a column, untitled. Its opening line was as clipped as a Boy's Own Annual: "Yesterday marked a day when speed exacted its price at Brooklands, as it will always do where men and women meet the future at forty miles an hour."

She read on. No flourish of disaster, no tongue for the carnage at the banking. It was, she noted, almost bloodless. The whole draft might have been prepared in advance, blank with placeholders for whichever 'thrilling' or 'ignominious' event the week served up. As for the crash, at least in this version, it was reported with the same dry resignation as a missed train or a change in the weather.

Mildred's lips pressed together in a thoughtful line. In the press tent, Brooks's fellow reporters had called him lucky and sly; they'd dropped hints about always being at the right place for catastrophe. But this column, for all its polish, did not have an air of rehearsal or secret foreknowledge. It was, if anything, underwhelming.

She tucked the draft back, just as Brooks returned, bearing a triumphant slice of toast and a twinkling eye. "Lady Ramsay! Robbery in the temple?"

"Merely searching for inspiration," she replied, raising an eyebrow at his plate.

"Let me know if you find any; some say my style's gone off since the war."

"Perhaps your style is too adaptable," Mildred answered, sending him a wry smile to blunt the accusation.

Brooks grinned, pleased as a fox. "Every story needs a little polishing, my lady."

Before the banter could deepen, the heavy tread of Rollo Sykes came to the door. The Club photographer, as always, looked faintly harried, his shirt-sleeves flashed with developer stains and his cuffs smelling faintly of vinegar and iodine.

Sykes carried a sheaf of glass plates, cradled against his chest. "Lady Ramsay, would you have a moment?" His gaze flickered uncertainly to Brooks, but he pressed on. "Inspector Kent wished for these to be seen by a neutral eye, and, as such, not a newspaper's reporter."

Mildred motioned for them both to sit at one of the heavy oak tables under the window.

"These are the best I managed to develop," Sykes explained, feverish with mixed pride and nerves. "The plates cover the banking, the paddock near the drum shed, and the run-up before Mallory's crash. Though I should mention, three negatives are still missing from yesterday's shooting."

He slid the plates across, one by one. The first: Rae St John, recognisable by her slight build and distinctive stride, standing far closer to the rail than she'd admitted, not three minutes before the incident. In the photograph, she faced away, but her stance and the marked curve of her helmet strap rendered the figure unmistakable.

The second: Victor Pym in close, urgent conversation with Alf Keating by the row of benzole drums. Sykes's lens caught them unaware; Alf turned half away, arms folded, while Pym's finger jabbed at a sheaf of papers. The air between them almost visibly crackled.

Next, a curiously artful image: the rear of the press tent, Brooks with camera to his eye, catching a candid moment of

Ivy Carrington's committee, while a mechanic darted through the background, almost a blur.

Kent appeared then, called by an earlier arrangement, and nodded approval as Mildred examined the images. "Each, as you see, is a moment open to interpretation," he said.

Brooks, lips set, found his stance more defensive. "My dear Sykes makes a habit of being where the drama can be posed, don't you?"

Sykes bristled. "Better posed than written after the fact. At least a plate can't be edited in the darkroom the way a story can be in the typewriter."

Brooks tutted. "You say that, Rollo, but you leave out how often photographers press the actors into their scene." He pointed to the plate featuring Rae. "She's closer there than she later claimed, yes, but who is to say she wasn't passing by, or that the precise moment is as unambiguous as it appears?"

Sykes retorted, "And the scene with Pym and Keating? You can see for yourself the agitation. I don't stage a raised voice or a threatening gesture."

Kent slid into the conversation. "Every witness becomes an actor when called upon, and every record, photographic or written, colours by the operator's hand. But our business is to seek the moment that cannot so easily be repainted."

Mildred regarded the photograph of Pym and Alf. "This one may show urgency rather than collusion, but in the swirl of the paddock, even a conference of peacekeeper and engineer can appear suspect."

Brooks tapped his fingers on the table, exasperated but intent. "There's no ill intent in my columns, Lady Ramsay. I use phrases like 'a day when speed exacted its price' precisely because every week, in this job, that's true somewhere. Most of the time, it means nothing—until tragedy strikes."

Sykes pursed his lips. "But context is everything, Brooks. Routines conceal many sins. Who's to say which pose is accidental, which real—the wire beneath the heel, the cable in the spares drawer, or the half-seen meeting at the petrol shed?"

Kent's smile was mirthless. "Experience teaches us that sometimes two men can interpret the same moment and both may be wrong."

Brooks retorted, "At least my drafts are harmless, doctors' platitudes about risk and reward. Unlike some, I don't go out of my way to create drama for the sake of a dramatic image."

Sykes's face reddened, but it was Mildred who balanced the matter. "Both the column and the plate are records, but neither is proof in itself. What matters is the habits around them, who stands where and why, who thought their conduct would escape record, and why."

There was a charged pause. Brooks glanced down, rubbing graphite from his thumb. "I'll say this, Lady Ramsay: reporters may angle words, but few have the means or desire to cut cables or slip wires. Our ink stains are public; our deadlines less so. If I were inclined to make mischief, I'd do so with a rumour, not a wrench."

Sykes shrugged. "I have my negatives and my bent plates. Would to God I also had a lens into the heart of the matter."

At this, Kent stood. "Negatives tell something, but not all. If these images show anyone with indisputable opportunity, it's only part of the web. As yet, every story still has its shadowed corner."

Brooks scooped up his copy, eyes flicking to Mildred. "My 'stock copy' will always sound like prophecy in hindsight, but it's written with the blandness required when one files a dozen transitions a month. If there's guilt to be found, it's not in my typescript."

Mildred returned his look, thoughtful but withholding judgement. "Perhaps not, Mr Brooks, but you might show me your original notes from the morning, who you saw, where you were, and so forth?"

"Of course, Lady Ramsay. My handwriting's far worse than my prose, I warn you."

A truce of sorts was reached as they fanned out, Kent off to corner yet another reluctant witness, Sykes to the darkness of his developing room, Brooks to scrounge more specifics from anyone not yet too wary of a reporter's questions.

Bea drifted in, breathless from another round of delicate interrogations in the Clubhouse. "Entire committee's twitching, Mildred. Ivy's refusing to host supper unless she gets the plates back from Sykes. Pym's been seen pacing the telephone box with Ada wringing her hands."

Mildred shared the images with her, recounting, "Nothing here yet amounting to indictment. Rae was closer than she said; Pym's row with Alf looked heated, but might be routine. Brooks's copy, if anything, was too impersonal. Yet, it is telling who works from habit, who from design."

Bea squinted at the plate of Rae. "She looks more lost than secretive. Everyone suspects her because she's never where people expect."

Mildred replied softly, "Which, of course, is why it's easier for the true saboteur to hide, pretending to be routine, while others are accused of simply not fitting in."

They shared a moment of companionable weariness. All the evidence—typed, photographed, whispered—was more tangled for its partiality than clarified. Yet, Mildred thought with quiet resolution, the killer's cleverness was running out of cover. Sooner or later, a pattern would appear among the staged moments and generic stories, a move or gesture or wire whose logic only the saboteur, however careful, would leave unvarnished.

Dusk threatened once again and the paddock's energy began to rise, as if darkness bred secrets too stubborn for the light. As she turned for the Clubhouse, Mildred resolved her mind on the only path left: ignore the drama, the staged images, the clever words and seek, instead, the unmarked actions that truly revealed the heart of guilt.

20

The oppressive mix of drizzle and threat that sat over Brooklands had, by mid-morning, begun to lift, though not enough to dispel the clinging sense that each detail was now dredged, not discovered, from the stubborn mud of memory and routine. Despite Dr Marsh's forensic precision and Kent's relentless interrogations, the facts of the case now seemed clearer only insofar as each pointed toward the same discomfort: too many plausible hands, too many tiny gaps in the net.

After her examination of Brooks's "stock copy" and Sykes's artful, equivocal plates, Mildred craved something straightforward, a fact untainted by performance or habit. As she found herself summoned by Edwin Hartley to the Clubhouse lounge, she nursed that hope as one might nurse a cup of tea: perhaps it would be enough to fortify, if not completely sustain.

Hartley was already stationed at a long table, his 'evidence' spread like a clerk's war map. There were padlocked time-sheets from the Club paddock, broadsides of the day's events, tea tickets punched and initialled with the Club's crest. His usual clockwork composure was, for once, marked by impatience: one foot tapped, and one of his pocket watches rested open on the baize.

"Lady Ramsay, thank you," he said crisply. Beside him, Inspector Kent paged methodically through a bundle of forms, while Mrs Pruett sat on a side chair, her battered wristwatch set beside a teapot and her bun tray nowhere in sight.

"For the Board and the Yard, and, not least, for my own sleep, let's see if time and cups can illuminate motive and movement," Hartley began, tapping the tea tickets with a pencil. "The last fifteen minutes before the crash: Brooks has claimed, and four journalists have affirmed, that he was on the footbridge with a steaming cup in hand at 11:28. Mrs Pruett says the same, yet her watch, as you see, differs by at least five minutes from my own."

Mildred, drawing up a chair, remembered Mrs Pruett's confession: "It always runs slow, love, so many hands, and never enough springs."

Mrs Pruett held up the crumpled ribbon of ticket stubs. "I remember, for I'd just burnt my thumb refilling the urn. Brooks was polite, near fidgeting, but he hadn't gone far when the commotion started. If my watch is off, I'll eat my apron."

Kent interjected, "With so many relying on Mrs Pruett rather than the tower clock, we risk ascribing precision to what's, in truth, a chorus of clockwork error. The footbridge is a nexus point; one emerges there from the press tent, paddock or rail depending on urgency or habit."

Hartley flipped to another sheet. "Yet, tea ticket 1345 is Brooks's, time-stamped, followed by tickets for two other reporters, their own movements only barely corroborated by the rest."

"So Brooks could have reached the footbridge earlier, or left it earlier, depending on whose watch we trust," Mildred mused.

"Indeed." Kent's tone was thoughtful. "The reporter with the best eye for an 'angle' now has the perfect ambiguity, present at the right place, the time flexible by half a kettle's boil."

Mrs Pruett, not to be left out, snorted. "If that's guilt, every member here's at fault for missed trains." She patted Hartley's shoulder for comfort. "We do our best."

It was then that a sharp rap on the glass signalled a newcomer: George Lane, the Club's smallest messenger but certainly its swiftest, his scurrying knees, forever clad in boyish short trousers, were legendary for speed. George was ushered in, cap askew, mud streaked up one shin, and eyes wide with a boy's delight at his own importance.

"I've the word, Lady Ramsay, same as I gave the Inspector," he declared, standing to attention more smartly than half the pit team could manage.

"Go on, George," Kent prompted with a smile meant to reassure.

"I was sent to the paddock with a message for Alf Keating, before the crash. Just as I got to the garages, I saw Miss St John legging it, proper sprint, cap flying, right toward the rail. She called over, 'Spanner for Keating!' and whipped past me carrying her toolkit. She was there at the fencing before the car smashed, heard the bang and about dropped my parcel."

Mildred frowned slightly. "And Alf, did you see him nearby?"

George shook his head. "Didn't see him straight then, but a

minute later, after folk started shouting, there he was at the far pit, arms in the air, cursing blue murder."

Kent made a note. "Thank you, George. Are you sure it was before the crash, not just after?"

"Certainly, sir. I've got the ticket from the stores, see?" He produced a dog-eared slip, time punched, and Hartley nodded, confirming the routine: every errand carried a ticket.

Hartley riffled the committee's supply ledger, tracking the comings and goings. "That aligns with the storekeeper's book. Spanners out, spanners in. And the footbridge set against that throws Brooks and Rae into sharp relief at the crucial three-minute window."

It made for an awkward confluence. Rae, when summoned and questioned, her posture tired but defiant, shrugged. "I fetched the spanner because there's never one close to hand in the heat of the day. Alf yelled he needed the number fourteen, something about a sticky linkage. I ran for it, found the toolkit in the store, and was at the rail by the time the noise started."

Alf, when told, turned red at the ears. "Didn't ask Rae for a spanner, not then. My toolbox was open at my feet. The last thing I'd want is her dashing about with all the press watching. Stubborn as ever, if she says it, maybe she misheard me asking for tea."

Even Rae, caught off guard, blinked. "Perhaps I anticipated the need. Or perhaps the day's chaos has muddled my memory. But I swear I was running to help."

Bea, listening as she entered bearing two cups of restorative cocoa, remarked quietly, "Odd, isn't it? How easily the memory bends, and how hard the truth is to pin even when everyone means well."

Mildred agreed. "Especially in a place governed by urgency and routine. In the space between the shouted order and the recalled errand, anyone could pass unnoticed."

Yet another thread tangled into the knot: Victor Pym's "errand." At that time, according to Ada Finch and fuel tickets, Pym sent Ada to fetch a technical catalogue from the storeroom, ostensibly to check a discontinued cable model. At nearly the same moment, his initials appear in Ivy Carrington's committee fuel ledger, signing for "inspector review" on two drums designated for the Ladies'.

Ivy herself, summoned briefly from her kingdom of orchids and perfect tea service, confirmed with unshakeable poise, "Our committee ensured that all supplies were available, as ever. Mr Pym was most attentive to the quality and safety of everything marked for demonstration. It's customary for the Club's visiting engineers to double-check, each with our permission, of course."

Hartley was less sanguine. "Committee fuel ledgers show a flurry of sign-outs just before the crash. If we're not careful, Lady Ramsay, we'll have the entire club on scrutiny for an innocent pail of benzole."

Pym, when confronted, replied—voice measured, just tinged with hurt pride—"Yes, I signed for access, as anyone on the safety demonstration was allowed to. Inspector Kent himself green-lighted my rounds. As for the storeroom, Ada can account for my presence. She manages the inventory, far better than I."

When Kent laid all these timings side by side, a picture came not into focus but into deeper fog. Brooks might have been on the footbridge, unless his tea was swallowed too quickly. Rae might have fetched a spanner for Alf that Alf denied requesting. Pym's "errand" ran perfectly alongside Ada's run to the storeroom, and Ivy's ledger, meticulous as ever, showed the committee's hands on fuel and supplies at every critical moment.

"Too many hands to pin," Bea murmured to Mildred as the noon bells struck, sending a fresh ripple of activity across the circuit. "Every clue corresponds to multiple alibis. Every errand might be genuine or a distraction."

Mildred, eyeing her notes, felt her own patience flicker. "If guilt hides here, it does so as a shadow behind perfect routine. The murderer counted on us tripping over these timing discrepancies, leaning too hard on plausible but shifting witness."

She drew Kent aside. "We know only this: the saboteur did not act outside the norm, but deep within it. Every movement that day, fetching tools, collecting tea, inspecting fuel, provided both cover and opportunity. If we wait for an undisputed timing, we may wait forever."

Kent nodded sombrely. "Then we must work with intent, not merely clockwork. Pressure each witness for details about habit and improvisation, not when, but why, and who benefits by the confusion."

Back in the main lounge, the usual comedy of late morning drama unfolded, drivers testing their stories against one another, Ada and Ivy's secretarial reserves pressed to the limits, even Mrs Pruett being besieged anew for reassurance.

Bea drew Mildred aside, her tone brightening as she pressed a biscuit into her hand. "If we ever solve it, darling, it'll be by knowing who relished improvisation, and who really trusted to habit. Time is an accomplice, and some people know it all too well."

Mildred, smiling in weary companionship, squeezed Bea's hand. "Then let's watch not the clocks, but the faces. For somewhere in the tangle, one pair of hands placed wire, forged tag, or cut cable, and trusted Brooklands's own routine to shield them."

And with that, as afternoon sunlight chased the mist, Mildred resolved that this time, she would not be tripped by clocks or kindness. If the murderer had gambled on confusion, they had not accounted for the possibility that someone would, at last, see not only the gaps in time, but the character in every quiet movement. The net, though crowded, was starting to tighten.

21

The autumn sun, limping through the haze, brought little cheer to Brooklands. By midday the circuit was busy but oppressed; people moving with a kind of cautious energy, every laugh a little brittle, every tale told with one eye on who might be listening.

After the fruitless reconciliation of timings and witness accounts earlier that morning, Mildred was determined to hunt for the physical, the unarguable. As the Club's lunch bell sounded, she broke away from the more public drama, drawing Bea with her to the sheds behind the Clubhouse kitchens, where empty fuel drums stood in a ragged formation and the scent of engine spirits coiled with a less savoury odour of frying onions.

It was here, wedged by crates but visible to any purposeful hand, that Mildred found the famous "benzole heavy" drum. Its label was pierced at the corners, tacked hastily, she noted, as if shifted and re-attached more than once. When Bea nudged it, it rolled sluggishly, a slosh audible inside.

"Benzole," Bea murmured, nose wrinkling. "I suppose if

you're bent on mayhem, you want to keep your flammable well-disguised."

"Except this didn't smell of anything at all, early on," said Mildred. "But now, see how the scent clings round the cap, the last hour, the warmth has brought it up." She caught a deep breath. "Almost masked. Kitchen smoke, perhaps? It must have drifted down from the exhaust vents. Enough to cover the odour for anyone hurrying."

A door banged. Smith, the Club supplies man, peered out, wiping his palms with a rag. "Nothing out of order, ladies?" His tone was always bland, yet Mildred noted the sidelong look he gave the drum.

"Thank you, Mr Smith," she replied smoothly. "We were told this drum was moved, perhaps mistakenly. Are you sure of the timing?"

He shrugged. "Early as I can recall, the committee were bustling around, and someone from the safety demonstration asked to check supply tags. Mr Pym, or maybe one of the juniors. Busy crowd, and the kitchen had vents open, smoke everywhere. Easy enough to lose a label in all that. I set the drum aside to settle any confusion."

Smith disappeared, already busy with new crises. Mildred crouched for a better look. This label was smudged by both ink and soot. If someone had swapped it, exploited the airflow of the Club's kitchen, and moved it twice in the hurry, perhaps it was never meant to be found until much later.

"Smoke screens literal and figurative," Bea mused.

"Quite," Mildred murmured. "Let's see how many have keys to the kitchen yard. The answer might point us to someone on more familiar terms with domestic confusion than mechanical."

THE MYSTERY OF THE FINAL LAP

Waving Bea on to keep an ear in the kitchens, Mildred cut through to the main house, climbing the back stairs to the upper floor, where a locked, glass-roofed sunroom stretched out above the west side of the Clubhouse. Long dubbed the Orchid Room for Lady Carrington's lavish hothouse displays, it was both sanctuary and subtle command post.

Today, the door was ajar. Maudie Knowles had left a watering can just inside, its trail damp on the tile. The air shimmered with moisture and floral sweetness, a world away from the grit and grease below. Potted cymbidiums and spiky phalaenopsis stood alongside paperwork and a locked ledger.

Mildred shut the door behind her, rifled methodically among the mail. Most was as expected—flower show catalogues and correspondence with nursery suppliers. However, between two invoices lay a carbon copy, unsigned but recently typed, a letter to an insurance underwriter.

She read:

My dear Mr Harrow, Thank you for expediting terms on the revised policy for the Ladies' Autumn Charity. As discussed, it is prudent to acknowledge the risk of 'inevitable accident or fatality where motor sport is involved'—our solicitors suggested this is unexceptional boilerplate. Please confirm coverage for all club officials, participants and committee members to the fullest extent should any such occurrence, God forbid, take place. I appreciate your prompt attention to these unforeseen necessities.

Yours with gratitude, I.C.

The date was striking: two days before Mallory's fatal crash.

Mildred's fingers tensed. Was this genuine committee business, practical, necessary insurance for a sport defined by risk or foreknowledge? The phrase "inevitable accident" carried a chill, its bureaucratic safety net suddenly loaded with a different significance.

Her thoughts were interrupted by the sound of a heel on tile. Lady Ivy Carrington herself entered, looking as composed as an orchid stem, every line in her silvery suit meticulously in place.

"Oh, Lady Ramsay! I trust the warmth is not too cloying. I was just checking on the oncidiums, they wilt if the vents are left too long. Shall I show you my newest?"

Mildred met her gaze, but with no preamble unfolded the letter. "I found this among your correspondence, Lady Carrington. Was there a specific reason for sending this insurance request two days before the demonstration crash?"

Ivy's pause was so slight only an old actress or a seasoned observer would have caught it. At once she produced the smile of the perfectly innocent. "Routine, my dear. The charity's legal advisers asked for confirmation of our coverage every year, since that terrible incident in '23, remember. The phrase is standard, wretched as it sounds. In a world where racing is perennially a near-fatal undertaking, one would be mad not to take precautions."

She folded her hands, palm over palm, unshaken. "I deeply regret the tone, but our solicitors are strict. Nor was any of this concealed, indeed, I circulated copies at the planning meeting. Ask Maudie."

Mildred chose her next words carefully. "You would acknowledge, perhaps, that the phrase reads oddly, after all that's happened."

Ivy's eyes remained unblinking. "I would acknowledge we are all the slaves of hindsight, Lady Ramsay. The committee's first duty is not only to the living, but to the club's continuity, its finances, its respectability. If tragedy occurs, we must at least be secure in safeguarding our members against ruin."

"It would also be a very effective shield," Mildred said, not unkindly. "And a signal to anyone, if there were such a person, that the risk is not only tolerable but planned against."

A shadow passed over Ivy's face, then was gone. "I plan for everything, Lady Ramsay. That is my burden, as you yourself surely know. Accidents are inevitable, but it is not my habit to profit by them. Nor, I hope, to be their cause. If there is suspicion, let there be clarity, however it hurts the institution."

She gestured to the begonia by the writing desk. "I am not the only one who understood Mallory's stance was inconvenient, perhaps to the club, perhaps even to the financial propriety of our sponsors. But my methods are always transparent. Would to God the world answered me in kind."

A brief silence lingered as Mildred weighed every syllable, truth, calculation, or just the measured poise of someone used to weathering all storms. Ivy pressed on, voice regulated.

"Please, take what you need. If I am to be doubted, let there be no locked rooms in my affairs."

Mildred nodded, placing the letter in her satchel. "Thank you, Lady Carrington. You'll understand we are pursuing every avenue, routine or otherwise."

Ivy straightened her lapel. "Track down every tag, every ledger, every club key. I will even lead the tour myself, if that is what is required. What I cannot control is what happens on the track, or in the hearts of the ambitious. You, I hope, believe me?"

Mildred looked her in the eye. "I believe you would never sacrifice Brooklands to scandal, Lady Carrington. But I also believe some people find even honest caution ambiguous when the worst comes to pass."

With a gleam of weary admiration, Ivy inclined her head. "That's the curse of leadership, Lady Ramsay. I bear it as best I can."

On departing, Mildred paused and glanced back at the profusion of orchids, delicate blooms that flourished in the warmth, their vitality protected by the vigilance of one determined woman.

Downstairs, Bea waited in the wide corridor, amusement meeting Mildred's returning gaze. "Did she reveal her villainy, or only the usual battery of insurance and disappointment?"

Mildred shook her head. "Neither. She displays her caution openly and disguises what, if anything, lies beneath. If this was all about certainty, perhaps the wrong line of questioning would undo it all."

The afternoon sun glanced off the Clubhouse panes as they made their way down the main steps. The air felt clearer, somehow; the accident's shadow had not lifted, but the day's practicalities, the drum, the odour, the possibility of confusion hiding intent, had thrown into relief the limits of careful documentation and prudent planning.

Mildred wondered, as she reflected on Ivy Carrington's unwavering composure, whether the true clue would lie not in a caught-out deceit, but in some flaw of expectation, in a routine too carefully observed, a risk too perfectly anticipated, an accident that, above all, was doomed to occur as if from the beginning.

Only a little more fire, one more test, one more question, would crack the shell. And then, perhaps, even the most splendid orchids would not escape the cold clarity of the autumn air.

22

The world was all washed silver and faint blue in the early morning, the great expanse of Brooklands lying empty and dew-laden beneath a sky that promised, at last, a measure of clarity. For once, Lady Mildred Ramsay had risen before the clatter of the kitchen teapots; even the circuit's mechanics had not yet roused themselves fully to grumble and bustle. She breathed in the cold, oil-damp air by the empty grandstand and saw only Rae St John, dressed in male-cut tweeds and a woollen cap, waiting beside the green Bentley beneath the softening haze.

"You came, then." Rae's voice, half-amused and half-challenging, carried in the hush. "Ready to see what those committee tea parties kept you from all these years?"

Mildred smiled ruefully. "I'm not convinced my nerves were ever intended for engines. But curiosity demands more than comfort."

Rae tossed her the gauntlet in the form of gloves. "Best way to chase theory is to chase tarmac first. Step in. I'll let you do the starting, if your courage holds."

They made a curious pair, Mildred stiff-backed, Rae loose-limbed and brisk in her teaching, as the car purred to life with a satisfying, throaty impatience. Mildred's hands were careful at the wheel, the memory of a war nurse's steadiness helping disguise the tremor. The pedals, wider and heavier than any motor car designed for gentlefolk, seemed an extension of Rae's challenge. Most daunting of all was the peculiar sense of exposure, the banking curves awash in mist, and the certain knowledge that the old habits of theory, deduction, and genteel observation would avail her little here.

"Right," Rae murmured, leaning close. "It's a test, you and the car. Don't fight it. Listen; let it guide you. Forty's your number, enough for a lesson, not enough for headlines or disaster."

"Am I in danger of either?" Mildred shot back, summoning a boldness she didn't quite feel.

"Only of exceeding your own limits." Rae reached across and reset the odometer. "Follow the straight, crest the footbridge, veer off at the press tent. Watch, every yard, every moment."

She obeyed, first tentatively, then, as Rae's confidence seeped into her, with increasing resolve. The car made its protestations quickly—brakes tight, transmission reluctant, a throttle more eager than mild. But in the slip of the rising sun and the arc of the banking, Mildred felt a clarity descend that was sharper even than observation. Every clatter and hiss was information: what a driver might feel, what a saboteur might exploit.

As they neared the footbridge, Mildred drew the car to a brisk stop, feet finally matching brain and balance. "This is faster than I would ever reasonably maintain for a committee schedule."

"Precisely," Rae said. "Mallory was more moderate than most, but even at full tilt, this is how long you'd have between sight lines, between being seen at the garages and vanishing beneath the eyes on the bridge, or in the press tent."

She checked the watch. "Two minutes and a half, from paddock to tent at forty. Take another loop, and keep your eyes to the sides. Imagine you're not merely driving, but that you wish to vanish. At speed, patterns disguise as routine."

This time, Mildred added intent to her journey. She pictured every possible theft of a glance: pockets of cover by the drum racks, gaps at the kitchen outflow, shadows behind the toolshed. She visualised the saboteur's hand dipping to the exposed brake cable during those seconds when even Brooks and Sykes would be distracted, scratching a sharp line, or, more cleverly, attaching a control wire beneath the pedal. With the cloud of routine and the smokescreen of breakfast, it would almost be easier than not.

At the press tent, she braked, this time relinquishing control with relief to Rae, whose approving nod felt more honest than many a committee commendation.

"Fifty yards of exposure," Rae said softly, "but only three to five seconds in view. The rest, yours to exploit, if you know the landscape."

They swapped places and idled for a moment beneath the shelter of the tent awning as the first hints of activity began across the circuit. Distantly, Mrs Thwaite's kitchen window yawned open, the promise of tea sailing across the yards.

Rae retrieved from the back seat a length of slender steel wire, a duplicate of the one used in Bea's recent "accident." She laid it across the dashboard, both challenge and proof.

"Here's your hypothetical: A clever hand, within that slot of two, three minutes, scores a cable, loops this wire beneath the pedal, and is away before the stewards ever dream there's business but breakfast. It isn't magic, just knowledge, boldness, and bluff."

Mildred eyed the wire, now profoundly ordinary in the morning light. "You mean to say any racer, any mechanic, even a certain sort of reporter, could achieve the trick? Not strength, not even special cruelty, just means and opportunity, a habit of routine?"

"Exactly," Rae replied, a touch of grim respect. "The club's routines are a shield and a weapon, both. To some, safety; to others, at best, camouflage."

A low cough from outside the passenger window announced Kent's arrival, his hat worn slightly askew as if to signal, privately, that not all was order in his day. He nodded at Rae, then met Mildred's gaze with a look both weary and quietly proud.

"Did you manage it?" he asked.

Rae's answer was brief, but Mildred's came with a glow of adrenaline. "I handled it." The words felt both true and metaphor: yes, she had managed the car, the route, even the fear. But more, she had now experienced, in her bones, how one could turn normality, safety itself, against an unsuspecting victim. It was not genius, just nerve and knowledge of the landscape.

Kent's eyes, always acute, softened. "Then you see how anyone, inside the club or out, could have done it. They need not be a villain by nature. They need not hate Mallory, or anyone; only need to have reason and the golden moment."

The three stood for a while in companionable silence as sunrise washed gold and rain-pale silver across the circuit. In this light, even the familiar looked new. For the first time, Mildred felt not only the weight of accumulated clues but the simultaneous burden and liberation of having physically tested the course. The investigation was no longer for her a question of "could it have happened," but "who felt permitted to do it, believing none would question their actions or presence?"

"I think," she said quietly, "we've been tricked not by a master criminal but by a master of routine, a person who believes, perhaps unconsciously, that their courage or cunning is always in service of the ordinary." She looked at Kent, realising the phrase applied not only to the murderer but alarmingly, perhaps reassuringly, to herself.

He smiled. "You controlled the car. You controlled the method. That's most of the battle."

Rae, drained but no less fierce, inclined her head. "And now the challenge, Lady Ramsay, is to control what comes next. Not luck, not guesswork. Courage, yes. But more—a refusal to let anyone else own the story."

Another engine started up nearby. The circuit was stirring fully now; voices wearing the preoccupied timbre of people preparing for another day of normality, even as the shadow of an unresolved murder lengthened behind them.

Mildred slid from the Bentley, feeling a new steadiness in her step. She was not now simply a watcher or interpreter; she had, if only for a bright moment in the dawn, joined the game on its own terms.

As they crossed back toward the paddock, Mrs Thwaite's call for tea rang out, strangely sweet and grave.

Bea met them at the garage doors, eyes bright with curiosity. "Did you break any records, or only the circuit's last remaining sense of order?"

Mildred laughed, feeling years younger for the effort. "Perhaps just a few illusions."

Bea pressed a hand over Mildred's glove. "The best kind to shatter, if you ask me."

The three exchanged a glance, each with new clarity, each carrying now, not just questions but living, tested answers. Routine could mask a crime or create an alibi, but it could also lay bare a pattern for a determined seeker. And Mildred, present, practical, and a little proud, was ready for whatever pattern the coming day would bring.

The murderer, she knew at last, had underestimated one crucial opponent, the courage of a woman willing to understand both the shape of danger and the subtle liberties of opportunity.

Onward, then, into the day, and toward the hidden resolution still burning quietly at the heart of Brooklands.

23

The sky above Brooklands had cleared to an almost indecent blue, the clarity a dissonant backdrop to the intricate, sometimes squalid work of unravelling the last knots of deception and routine. Mildred, fortified by her dawn drive and the rare sweetness of purpose, found herself once more at the heart of the Club's warren, along with half the cast of her recent suspicions, and a constable with a bashfulness that even his new boots could not disguise.

Constable Freddie Blake intercepted her in the corridor, hat in hand and with an air of shy triumph about him. "Lady Ramsay? I believe I've found something that, the Inspector thought, well, you should see first."

She followed him into the Club's chilly, underlit archive, a room that smelled of polish and old telegrams. On the wide central table sat an unremarkable stationery envelope, brown, with a blue stamp and a corner peculiarly foxed, as if it had once been worried by nervous fingers or damp air. Blake tipped the envelope: nothing inside.

He explained, voice low and careful, "Turned up in the wastebasket by the darkroom, ma'am. Label shows Brooks's supplier, see there? Same shade, same grain as those pads of his." He hesitated. "But look here, these foxed corners match Rae St John's outgoing correspondence." He'd already laid her last, crumpled post beside it: a fingerprint at the tip, the spatter of rain or sweat on the edge.

Mildred ran her thumb over the mark. Letter, envelope, both slightly water-stained, both bearing traces of ink now so smeared as to be almost illegible. There was a faint, tell-tale whiff—smoke, chemicals, and perhaps a hint of the lavender Ivy Carrington favoured for her stationery drawer.

It might have been nothing: a mechanic's mishap, an incautious pressman's empty, discarded sleeve. But in this tight final act, even the most innocent paper felt faintly redolent of blackmail. And motive thrived on overlaps.

"A missing negative, or an incriminating note?" Mildred asked.

Blake, ever the diligent, shook his head. "Club darkroom confirms those same three plates still haven't been logged. Sykes accounted for a misplaced close-up that showed nothing... but he was short an envelope. Brooks claims he saw the missing set briefly yesterday evening. Rae herself posted some letters in a hurry; denies losing anything, but is jumpy as a wet cat."

"Whose writing matches the western edge here?" Mildred pressed.

Blake cleared his throat, awkward. "Closest is Brooks. He edges his envelopes flat by habit, club porters say. But the foxing... well, that's common this week. The air's been damp, and the bins leak."

He hovered as she took a last whiff of the strange, mixed scent. "If you ask me, ma'am, somebody tucked something, negative or letter, into this, walked the wrong way around the bins, panicked, and threw it out. Might have been confiding, might have been blackmail."

She pocketed the envelope. "The scent of a coward, or a conspirator, Constable. Either way, it tells us something worth chasing."

This new uncertainty led her, after a brisk detour through the Club's garden, to the communal writing room. It was, inevitably, a chaos of half-written notes, old typewriter ribbons, and secretarial supplies. At its heart, the Club's battered communal typewriter sat misused and mortally abused—its ribbon stretched taut, keys worn to the bone. This, Mildred knew, was both the instrument of the official minutes and the confessions, warnings and plots of half the players in her drama.

Today, though, the carriage wasn't locked. A fresh, blackened ribbon lay beside the machine. Mildred, with a habit's precision, slid a used one from the bin and examined it under the reading lamp. She called to Kent, who, summoned by her note, now slipped into the room.

"What is it?" he murmured, seeing her peering at the winding, coal-dark strip—his face full of that restrained eagerness she'd come to trust.

"Multiple heavy strikes," she whispered, passing him the ribbon with tweezers. "See here, the letters 'D,' 'A,' 'N,'— hammered in, not tapped gently as a secretary might have done. Some words—'danger,' 'withdraw,' even a stray 'die'— appear to have been typed with urgency—or force."

Kent frowned, tracing a finger down the ribbon. "The letters are deeper, the force uneven. Not the careful work of someone composing minutes, or Ada's usual script. This could be Brooks—he types with unnecessary energy. Or Pym, who's heavy-handed, according to Ada. Even Ivy's secretary, Maudie, though her hand is muscled by files not stories."

Mildred considered. "The warning letters Mallory received could have come from anywhere. The wording stings, but the style is vanilla, anonymous, rehearsed. Someone typed the first gently, but a second or third, less a warning than a threat, pressed harder. Frustration, panic, or loathing... the emotion is literally imprinted, not just composed."

At that moment, Ada Finch appeared in the doorway, her face pale, her handbag clutched tightly as a child with a cold. "Excuse me," she whispered. "Was I wanted? If you're examining the ribbons, Lady Ramsay, I... I should explain about the letter."

Kent gave a reassuring nod, but Mildred was gentle, offering Ada a seat by the window.

"You typed a note for Mr Pym. But did you compose the second—stronger, more pointed?"

Ada's hands twisted together in her lap. Her voice dropped to an anxious hush. "Mr Pym asked me to warn Captain Mallory. That's all. Something about not criticising safety products in public. I typed it, a 'professional courtesy' he called it, on the Club machine, because my Remington was out. But"—she steadied herself—"I left the ribbon in, didn't rewind it, and stepped away to fetch him the cable catalogue from the files."

She paused, shame riding her features. "Anyone could have used the machine before I returned. Brooks sometimes dashed off lines there after lunch; Miss Maudie finished up invoices for Ivy; even Sykes wrote captions for his galleries at that desk."

Kent pressed. "Did you see anyone else in the room?"

Ada shook her head, eyes full of dread. "No, but I heard someone. Footsteps, a faint, heavy typing, like the clack my father made after strong drink. I thought nothing of it—until the talk spread of blackmail and real threats."

Mildred took her hand. "What you've described enables, but does not accuse. Inexperience is no crime, perhaps only what the schemer hoped to exploit."

Ada let a breath escape, as if she had been holding it for a week. "I'm so sorry, Lady Ramsay. If… if my act let someone escalate a 'courtesy' into something cruel…"

"That's exactly the sort of small negligence the murderer counted on," Mildred said softly. "But if you remember something more—words, anyone returning to the desk—tell us."

Ada nodded, then hurried out, shoulders hunched inward.

Kent's face set into hard lines. "We know now the warning letter was genuine, a nudge rather than a threat. But someone, in the same hour, built on it, using Ada's presence and distraction to type a far harsher note and seed fear. They chose a ribbon already loaded with anxiety. The question, Lady Ramsay, is—who had the most to gain by escalating a warning into a threat?"

Mildred reviewed the envelope once more, felt the texture of both eagerness and anxiety. "Anyone who needed leverage: Brooks for a story, Pym for reputation, Ivy for insurance, Rae to remove an obstacle, Maudie—perhaps even Alf if blackmail or protection was needed." She said it deliberately, watching Kent's mouth tighten.

"Yet all the evidence is circumspect, shadows in a haze of routine. Every person here can, by accident or design, appear to have both access and motive."

They reviewed the envelope again. The foxed corner matched Rae's hand, but the type and ribbon more closely matched Brooks's requirements. Mr Pym, heavy-handed with his paperwork, could as easily have dashed off a warning as an editor a column. Ivy's secretaries, thorough and methodical, could type anything with dry efficiency.

The final piece of the pattern was now clear: the stolen negatives we'd recovered from Brooks's portfolio. Sykes's plates, once catalogued with meticulous care, had revealed the deception. Those critical moments—Rae near the rail, Pym and Alf among the drums—had been deliberately removed, the evidence temporarily hidden by the simplest ruse: slip the plate out, slip in something else, and the envelope appears untouched.

Kent closed the box of ribbons and negatives with finality. "The next conversation will not concern clocks or cables. We must search for habit, who walks the route, who claims anxiety over deadlines, who composes threats with two strikes rather than one."

Mildred nodded. "And soon, we must provoke a new, unscripted response: force their hand in front of all, and see who cannot improvise without giving themselves away."

She glanced outside, where the circuit was now flooded with noon, its light both exposing and full of shadow. The day pressed onward, the final net tightening over Brooklands.

In that bright coldness, Mildred felt the story's tension unmistakably pulling taut: every message, every photograph, every line of type now weighted with meaning. The saboteur had counted on clubs and habits and unsuspicious moments. But the investigation, at last, was about to become the one thing that routine could not anticipate—a test of character on an open stage, impossible for the guilty to rehearse.

24

By late afternoon, a distinctly autumnal clarity hung over Brooklands, cut through with a bracing wind that sent committee women reaching for their shawls and mechanics hurrying to secure their toolboxes. The circuit's routines wavered between the fierce comfort of habit and the trembling edge of exposure; for Mildred, the day had become an exercise in closing nets, no longer about possibilities, but about truths waiting to be forced unvarnished to the surface.

After the business with the missing negatives and the communal typewriter, and a flurry of short, significant interviews, Mildred found herself eyeing Victor Pym across the deserted Clubhouse lounge. He was going through folders and bills at a far table, the backdrop of orchids and the faint scent of polish only underscoring his discomfiture. Mildred had learned by now that nothing disconcerted Pym so much as the whiff that his paperwork might not be his own affair.

She made her approach with the lightness of one who owns the ground she walks on. "Mr Pym, I see the day has not let you rest. Nor, it seems, have your ledgers."

He snapped the last folder shut, but she noted the tension in his jaw. "Lady Ramsay. If you've come, as Kent has, to examine every receipt, I beg you'll look first at the debits. We are all, every vendor here, balancing reputation against solvency."

"Well then," Mildred replied gently, "let's speak plainly. I have reason to believe some of your outlays are not, strictly speaking, for materials. Here, for example—" she tapped the marked line in his ledger, "—'Special services,' outlayed weekly, paid in cash to a 'Mr H.' Not an engineer, I take it?"

Pym's veneer slipped, just briefly, into petulance. "If you must know, that's Hobson, the bookmaker's runner. It is common—well, club custom—for us sometimes to deal in incentives to smooth the ruffled edges of the paddock. It is not corruption. It is… reputation management, in a noisy business."

"Reputation management?" Mildred echoed, her tone deliberately mild.

He squirmed. "There are drivers and… others who can be difficult, when pressed by debts. Small tokens, reminders, a little hush money, it's not so much bribery as preserving programme harmony. No one wishes the Board or committee to be embarrassed by public quarrels, or, heaven help us, a scene over a lost bet."

He seemed desperate for sympathy or complicity. "Lady Ramsay, if all debts were aired, races would be run in silence. Surely you see how delicate it is; one cannot always afford a scandal halfway through the season."

Mildred nodded, allowing herself a flicker of realism. "But wouldn't such delicacy encourage more cunning forms of blackmail, Mr Pym?"

THE MYSTERY OF THE FINAL LAP

His mouth twitched. "Perhaps, if one is unwise. But if it means avoiding a spectacle, well, that is the greater good here, surely?"

She let him have the illusion of agreement, just long enough to note which vouchers he was most careful to shuffle away. With a nod, she moved into the hall, where the club's latest drama was gathering for its next act.

Already Bea had secured the rattled Mr Hobson, a lanky, smoke-stained man with a battered runner's cap and a wallet fat with folded slips. He perched on the edge of one of Mrs Thwaite's Windsor chairs in the refreshment annex, obviously awaiting no joy.

Beside him, stiff and embarrassed, stood Alf Keating, sleeves rolled, face red. The tension between them was enough to put sparks on the tartan carpet.

Bea caught Mildred's eye. "Mr Hobson has a recollection that runs counter to the circuit's norms for discretion."

Mildred sat and offered a gentle smile. "Mr Hobson, I believe you have some perspective on the recent exchanges, loans and such?"

Hobson coughed and shot Alf a wary look. "I do, ma'am. No disrespect to the gent, but, Keating here came to me a fortnight back, desperate for a few quid. Said he'd clear it soon as any proper payout came. But then, when I asked why so hasty, he said: 'If a spectacle comes off, it'll all be square, maybe more than square, if the right sort of accident unfolds.'"

A collective hush. Alf's fists curled at his side. "Rubbish," he hissed. "I never said any such thing! I asked for a short loan, that's all. Cover my losses till payday. I never wished for, or planned, anything to do with crashes or money for a man's life!"

Hobson shrugged, but his eyes darted. "I'm only the messenger, Mr Keating. But you did say the word 'accident'—and I don't forget talk that rings odd."

Inspector Kent, hovering in the corner, stepped closer. "Would this be a regular arrangement, Mr Hobson—loans to paddock staff, repayment upon... what, insurance payouts? Winnings?"

Hobson bristled. "People pay what they owe, one way or the other. Sometimes there's talk, sometimes it goes no farther. But this time, well—" Here he hesitated. "I'll say I was encouraged to mention the business at the Club when questions started flying. Not by this man"—jerking his head at Alf—"but by someone anxious to keep attention off other runners in the field."

Mildred closed in softly: "Encouraged how, Mr Hobson?"

He shuffled. "Told there'd be a little something extra if I made sure to put Keating's name forward. Anonymous tip, stuck in my hat with a tenner. Nothing more was said, and I'm not much for making enemies."

A loaded silence. Alf's anger was now edged with humiliation. "You let yourself be used to muddy me up. I'll have the truth out, if I have to fight half the betting ring to get it."

As tempers escalated, Bea produced what she had saved for this very moment: the note from Captain Mallory, discovered in his pocketbook, complete with the paid IOU. Her timing was exquisite.

She laid it out for both men to see. "Gentlemen, perhaps this will clear the last of the bad blood. Captain Mallory settled Alf's outstanding account before the demonstration. You can check the handwriting, the date, the amount. There was no incentive left for Alf to be involved in anyone's accident nor reason for him to see restitution through disaster."

Alf glowered, but his tension visibly slackened. "He did me that kindness, it's true. There was nothing left to pay, except to my own shame for needing it."

Kent read the note, nodded, and folded it gently. "That, Mr Hobson, should resolve the doubts about motive. Our interest now concerns only those who sought to smear Alf, or draw suspicion away from themselves through your discretion."

Hobson was unmoved, but his shoulders dropped. "I never liked being in the thick of it, ma'am. But everyone must pay their rent. I'll say only that the tip to muddy Keating came from a note in a club envelope, left for me with my usual. There were gloves' marks on it—soot, maybe graphite, like a mechanic's paw or a reporter's hurry."

Mildred's eyes narrowed. "Not a committee hand, then?"

"No, ma'am. But clever enough to pay in cash and ask little in return."

Kent's brow furrowed. "If you ever decide to name the one who bought your silence, let us know. Meanwhile, I'll tell you: interfering in a murder inquiry with false witness draws more than petty inconvenience."

Hobson tipped his cap. "I'm just the messenger. That's all I'll say."

The small crowd began to disperse, mutters trailing as Alf left with a mixture of relief and exhausted fury. Mildred lingered with Bea and Kent in the annex, examining the ledgers and carefully considering motive and means.

Bea exhaled sharply. "So many strings, all tugged by hands that fear the light."

Kent offered a wry smile. "We may never have every name in every ledger, but the chief suspicion has now shifted."

Mildred nodded. "We know now Alf was meant to be a scapegoat, his debts cleared before the accident, but someone tried hard to paint him as desperate for 'a spectacle payout.' That smells not only of blackmail but of a diversion, a layer of performance built for the crowd and paper-trail alike."

Bea quietly added, "And the one who pushed Hobson to it, clever enough to use club envelopes and the residue of the circuit, not the polish of committee."

A hush settled, not altogether uncomfortable, at last, the noise of accusation was being replaced by the quiet, stubborn press of truth. There were, Mildred realised, only so many hands with the habit of cash and grime, only so many who understood the theatre of misdirection well enough to orchestrate such a smear.

One by one, the performers were exhausting their material; only the final act, she suspected, would truly require improvisation. The circle had shrunk: Mallory's uprightness precluded accident, Alf was cleared by both ledger and intent, and the killer, emboldened but desperate, must now fear that the next question, the next ledger, would be the last their confidence could weather.

As dusk fell and the Clubhouse lamps flickered on, Mildred squeezed Bea's hand. "Tomorrow... tomorrow, we end it," she whispered.

And in that moment, with the wind rattling the windows and the papers shifting at last toward honesty, Mildred was certain Brooklands would soon be free. If only the courage to face the last, most dangerous truth could hold through the oncoming night.

25

A morning as crisp as a bun's crust dawned over Brooklands, promising, at last, the decisive clarity that all the Club's caution and confusion had so thoroughly undermined. Lady Mildred Ramsay, who had slept very little and planned too much, found herself up before sunrise to orchestrate the day's unorthodox pursuit of justice. This day would not rely on rumour, on witness, or even on the too-forgiving partiality of routine. Today, Brooklands would walk straight into its own deception.

There was, Mildred privately thought as she buttoned her coat, something both theatrical and deeply proper about staging a reenactment. If the Club's labyrinthine habits had hidden the saboteur for this long, then only a controlled performance, with new props and old routines, could draw out the truth. She was, she realised with a glint of amusement, assembling the cast for one final show: a trap, baited with lampblack and bun crumbs, to catch a killer who thought themselves the master of both.

The morning began in the paddock, where Rae St John, steady-handed, looking only faintly weary, waited by a freshly tuned Humber, its brake cables gleaming. Mildred had insisted on a pristine part, installed in full view and under Hartley's closest supervision. She herself had, with a schoolgirl's excitement, borrowed a vial of lampblack from the Club's stores; Rae and Hartley dusted the cable's sleeve and anchor points lightly, leaving a film that might remain invisible to casual glances but would betray the touch of any hand in the attempt to tamper or erase.

"This way," Mildred murmured as she dusted, "our villain will either stain themselves, revealing where only innocence should tread, or leave a handprint so distinct even Inspector Kent will not miss it."

Hartley, twin pocket watches at the ready, arranged his stance as though he were timing the Derby and a bank robbery at the same time. "We shall trace every yard and second, Lady Ramsay. When Rae sets out, I will start the first. The second keeps the time for the opposite route— anyone returning after a furtive errand, or who wishes a word at the pedal, will find their times indefensible. Dr Marsh, ready?"

In keeping with the singular event (and perhaps the Club's theatrical bent), Dr Verity Marsh stood nearby, her medical valise open beside her seat on the pit wall. She looked, Mildred thought, rather like the calm observer to an amateur conjuring trick, not cynical, exactly, but ready for sleight-of-hand.

At the far edge of the paddock, Mildred stationed Bea and Mrs Pruett at a hastily erected bun stall, right beside the press tent, ostensibly to lift spirits and fortify the witnesses. In truth, bun and tea would function as a secondary snare. The plan was beautifully English and gently ruthless: every excuse to linger or slip away would be quietly logged, down to the last currant.

"When the starting gun sounds—" Mildred whispered, squeezing Bea's hand as final instructions flitted between bun wrappers—"watch who takes what, and most especially, who returns a little too breathless, lured perhaps by gossip, perhaps by greed."

Mrs Pruett, who had spent her lifetime observing men get up to secrets between the sugar and the urn, beamed at her new role as lookout. "If anyone doubles back for a second, I'll give them a receipt," she promised.

Meanwhile, Mildred's final stratagem was quietly seeded in the glassy orchid room atop the Clubhouse. She had secreted a forged insurance "addendum"—drawn up with Bea's skilled hand and just the right hint of legalese, amongst Ivy Carrington's ledgers, with a whisper to Maudie Knowles that the committee's insurance affairs might need "urgent review." The bait was subtle: the kind of paperwork that only someone with a reputation to lose would move to destroy, alter, or "clarify." Ivy's calm might be unshakable, but it was not, Mildred reckoned, impervious.

With the probabilities suddenly in motion, all that remained was to set the wheels in turn. Rae, looking both pleased and faintly exasperated, received her final orders with a grin. "A demonstration with an audience, and you want me to play the part of the not-quite-innocent?"

"Not so much a role as a rite of passage," Mildred replied, eyes twinkling. "You will drive from here past the press tent, at a steady forty, then loop through the garages, take a brief stop at the footbridge, and return. Hartley will log every second."

"And if someone tries for the cable?"

Hartley's voice, dry as old rye, filled the gap. "They'll find Dr Marsh and myself close at heel. And that cable"—he glanced at the lampblack—"will keep secrets better than a club porter with a tip."

The circuit was conspicuously crowded; Brooks, scenting drama, hovered by the press tent, notepad poised. Sykes fiddled with his camera, angling for "the exclusive angle" Mildred had promised—a slightly salacious hint that perhaps Ivy's insurance was to be publicly scrutinised or that the demonstration would reveal a new lapse in safety. More than one mechanic, after days of anxiety, could not resist the prospect of free buns, a race, and a hint of scandal.

The whistle blew.

Rae set off, smooth and purposeful, the Humber humming up the gravel. Hartley clicked the first watch. As planned, activity surged at the bun stall, a sudden demand for Mrs Pruett's best, and, notably, an immediate clustering of the younger journalists and committee volunteers. Sykes, in pursuit of his "angle," twice circled to the garages, glancing up at the Clubhouse windows. Brooks, after a word with a rival, disappeared briefly, excusing himself for a special feature interview.

Mildred, half-observer, half-target, roved the route: she noted greasy shadows at the garages, a small commotion near Pym's demonstration case, and, through a convenient window, Maudie Knowles poring over Ivy's files as Lady Carrington herself hovered, restive and noble, by the orchids.

As Rae returned, a minute under the expected time, thanks to her confidence on the banking, Hartley logged the precise duration. Rae popped out of the car, hands and gloves pristine, face amused. "No ghosts at the controls this time, Lady Ramsay. And no contestants at the brake, though our audience was rather too eager for the bun segment."

"Did anyone approach the car, heart in mouth for a tweak at the cable?" Dr Marsh asked.

"None," Rae replied firmly. "I kept my gaze in both mirrors, and Hartley's shadow was never far from the rear wing."

The pit, the cable, and the pedal were now due for inspection. Hartley, with gloves on, detached the brake cable and ran a swab of spirit across the lampblack film. To his satisfaction, a distinct thumb-smudge marred the dust at the anchor—fresh, pressed faintly, but too recent to be written off as casual equipment handling.

Kent approached, notes already prepared. "Let's see the timing, the notes from Mrs Pruett, and the crowd's positions. The thumb's orientation—right-handed, left-facing. Not Rae's, certainly, nor any of the mechanics nearby. Not Sykes or Brooks, who were both at the press tent for much of the interval, with buns and gossip."

Bea grinned. "And I can swear they both returned with jam on their cuffs, not lampblack."

Dr Marsh, careful as ever, confirmed that the smudge matched neither Rae nor the mechanics' prints on file. Forensics would follow, but for the moment the field had narrowed.

That left the second half of Mildred's trap. In the orchid room, Ivy was discovered safeguarding her ledgers, with Maudie anxiously relabelling files. The bait, the insurance "addendum"—was gone when Mildred performed her "routine" check half an hour later. Ivy was, of course, calm; she had the document in her hand and explained, with perfect composure, "One can't be too careful. Since you yourself said it was urgent..."

Bea, sidling up, whispered, "Fish on the line, or fisherman reeling their own catch a little too smoothly?"

Hartley, alerted, placed Mrs Pruett's bun stall receipts, Rae's lap times, and the thumbprint log on the green baize table in the Clubhouse library, now transformed into a war chamber. Kent and Mildred analysed the order of arrival, fading smears, and anxious glances.

"There were enough distractions," Kent murmured, "that only one with routine access, and real confidence in the machinery, would risk a stray smudge, even as the net closed."

Mildred nodded. "And the greed for control is, as ever, the fatal flaw. Our villain found the lampblack, thinking to erase it, but merely marked themselves more clearly."

As the day wore on, the bun stall's supplies dwindled, but the sense of approaching denouement only sharpened. The crowd sensed it too: less amusement, more speculation. Ivy maintained her poise even as she watched others with a predator's consideration. Brooks and Sykes argued over timeline and "angles," but both had alibis harried by tea and bun crumbs. Pym hovered at the margin, pale and intent, fingering cables whose innocence had finally been restored.

By evening, with the whistle of the last train in the air, Mildred faced her circle, friends, suspects, and strangers alike, and felt the particular serenity that comes with outwitting those who think themselves cleverer than justice. The trap had been set and sprung; now all that remained was to let the compelled confession, or the panic of exposure, bring down the curtain.

"Tomorrow," she promised Bea and Hartley as she tidied away slips and gloves, "we reveal the hand that wrote these routines, and the one who tried to erase them, too."

Brooklands would not, perhaps, be made entirely safe by truth. But by courage, bun crumbs, and the grimy theatre of a well-laid plan, it might once again be honourable. Mildred, hands unshaken but heart steady, was ready for the final unmasking.

26

The air at Brooklands seemed charged with a peculiar electricity that morning, a certain tautness that spoke of conclusions drawing near. The paddock's usual cheerful chaos had softened to watchful wariness; even the press tent's typewriters clacked with uncharacteristic restraint. Lady Mildred Ramsay, after a solitary breakfast and a meaningful conference with Dr Marsh and Inspector Kent, set the stage for what she knew must be the final act.

The Clubhouse library—all polished mahogany and leather-bound racing annuals—had been arranged with careful thought: a long table at the centre, chairs in a loose semi-circle, and a silver tray of buns (Mrs Thwaite's contribution to justice) set discreetly to one side. Hartley stood by the mantel, pocket watches laid before him like sacred relics. Dr Marsh had positioned herself by the window, her medical case open, a stack of evidence folders beside her. Kent, impassive as granite, waited at the head of the table.

They arrived in waves, first the committee members, with Ivy Carrington sailing in like a galleon in powder blue, her face betraying nothing but the faintest curiosity. Then came Victor

Pym, Ada at his elbow, his fingers compulsively straightening his cuffs. Sykes slipped in with his camera, nodding warily to Rae St John, who entered with her usual stride; purposeful, unapologetic. Last came Brooks, carelessly elegant as always, a pencil tucked behind his ear and his notebook open, as if he were merely covering another society function.

When all were seated, Mildred caught Kent's eye and gave a slight nod.

"Ladies and gentlemen," Kent began, his voice measured, "thank you for your attendance. As you know, yesterday's demonstration provided us with new evidence regarding Captain Mallory's death. It is now clear that his accident was neither misfortune nor mechanical failure, but a deliberate act of sabotage."

A ripple of reaction swept the room, Ivy's eyebrow arched, Pym's fingers twitched, Rae's jaw tightened. Only Brooks seemed untouched, scribbling a note with the air of a man recording someone else's tragedy.

"The brake cable used in yesterday's demonstration," Kent continued, "was dusted with lampblack, a substance invisible to casual observation but revealing to any hand that touched it. At the conclusion of the test, a clear thumbprint was found impressed in the lampblack near the cable's anchor point."

Hartley stepped forward. "This print, ladies and gentlemen, was left during the eight-minute window when Rae St John was performing her circuit. Someone approached the vehicle when it was unattended, touched the cable, and left their mark."

Sykes shifted uncomfortably. "Surely anyone might have brushed against it—a mechanic checking, or—"

"No mechanic was authorised to touch the assembly," Hartley

cut in. "No driver needed to adjust it. The print is an intrusion, not a necessary touch."

Dr Marsh now took her turn. "More significantly, we found this." She held up a folded handkerchief in gloved fingers. "This contains not only lampblack from our trap, but traces of graphite, the same graphite dust found on the original sabotaged cable from Captain Mallory's car. Not oil, not grease, but the fine, distinctive residue found in certain mechanical instruments."

All eyes in the room shifted warily. Pym cleared his throat. "Many of us handle graphite. Engineers, mechanics—"

"But few of us," Mildred interjected softly, "carry it on our hands from the press tent to a brake cable at the precise moment needed for sabotage. Fewer still would have access to the right gauge of wire to jam a pedal, or the expertise to score a cable just enough to ensure failure on the banking, not before."

Ivy's voice was cool. "You have a suspect, clearly. Why not name them?"

Kent nodded. "We tracked the movements of everyone present yesterday using Hartley's twin watches and Mrs Pruett's bun stall as timing posts. Only three people left their designated areas during the critical window, and returned with changed appearances."

A tight silence gripped the room. Pym's face had paled considerably. Rae sat utterly still. Brooks continued to write, his expression betraying only professional interest.

Hartley consulted his notes. "Mr Pym was observed at the telephone box for three minutes, then returned to his demonstration stand. Lady Carrington was seen entering the orchid room, where our falsified insurance 'addendum' had been placed, a document which subsequently disappeared."

He paused meaningfully. "And Mr Brooks left the press tent shortly after the start of the demonstration, returning eight minutes later with, according to Mrs Pruett's tally, an uneaten bun and a smudge on his right cuff that had not been there before."

At this, Brooks looked up, his pencil stilling. "I went to make a call. The London desk needed copy by noon."

"The telephone box was occupied by Mr Pym," Mildred said quietly. "And your handkerchief, Mr Brooks, tells a more specific story."

For the first time, uncertainty flickered across Brooks's features. "A handkerchief proves nothing, everyone at Brooklands comes away streaked with something."

"Not everyone," Dr Marsh replied, "carries both lampblack and the distinctive graphite found in camera shutters, the same graphite that stained Captain Mallory's brake cable."

A heavy silence descended. Rae's shoulders relaxed a fraction. Pym's breathing grew more regular. Only Brooks remained unnaturally still, his practiced nonchalance now clearly requiring effort.

Mildred moved to the centre of the room. "The circle has narrowed considerably since we began. Rae's graphite smudges were from throttle linkage practice, not sabotage. Pym's alleged bribe was indeed planted, his ledgers revealing only an excess of caution, not criminal intent. Lady Carrington's insurance letter proved to be standard practice, prudent rather than prescient. The supposedly 'bad' cable in Alf's drawer was merely a teaching tool used to show apprentices what to avoid."

She paused, letting the weight of exoneration settle before continuing.

"But there remained one person with both means and opportunity—someone who understood timing well enough to be perpetually in the right place at the crucial moment. Someone with access to fine wire of the exact gauge needed to temporarily jam a brake pedal, and the mechanical knowledge to score a cable just enough to ensure its failure under stress. Someone who would benefit professionally from a spectacular accident, and who had prepared a 'stock' article containing the phrase 'a day when speed exacted its price'—before any price had been paid."

All eyes turned to Brooks, whose face had drained of its usual animation.

Kent stepped forward, producing a length of slender wire. "This was found in your equipment bag, Mr Brooks, a camera shutter release cable, cut to precisely the length needed to wedge beneath a brake pedal during warm-up. When tested against the scoring on Mallory's cable, it matched perfectly."

"You can't seriously..." Brooks began, but his voice lacked conviction.

"When we examined your portfolio," Mildred continued, "we found those missing negatives from Sykes's darkroom. Images you'd removed not because they incriminated others, but because they showed you near the paddock at times that contradicted your alibis. The communal typewriter ribbon revealed you had retyped and intensified the warning letters to Captain Mallory, transforming Pym's cautious 'professional courtesy' into something far more threatening."

Hartley laid his watches on the table with finality. "Your timing, Mr Brooks, was always too perfect. When we checked Mrs Pruett's slow clock against mine, we found you consistently disappeared just before incidents, reappearing with camera ready when catastrophe struck. Not luck, design."

For a moment, Brooks seemed to consider denial, but the accumulated evidence appeared to crush his resistance. His shoulders slumped.

"It wasn't meant to kill him," he said finally, his voice hollow. "Just a skid—a dramatic moment for the camera. Racing needed a wake-up call about safety, and Fleet Street needed selling copy. My career was stalling; they wanted blood and thunder, not polite race reports."

The room exhaled collectively; shock, vindication, and relief mingling in the air.

Brooks continued, words tumbling faster now. "I timed it perfectly—the wire would dislodge after the warm-up lap, causing a skid, some drama for the crowd. The scoring was just insurance, to make it look like equipment failure. Mallory would have walked away with a tale to tell. But he hit the pedal harder than I expected, the wire released too soon, and the banking—" He broke off, unable to finish.

Rae's voice cut like steel. "And afterwards? When a man lay dead?"

Brooks couldn't meet her gaze. "By then, I was in too deep. I tried to muddy the waters, leave graphite traces near likely suspects, escalate the warnings to implicate Pym, suggest Alf had debts. I used the Club's own habits against it, the routines, the overlapping alibis. I knew how to make everyone look equally suspicious."

Kent moved forward. "You exploited the trust of an entire community for a headline, Mr Brooks. You took a man's life for the sake of your byline."

"I never meant—" Brooks began.

"To kill?" Mildred finished softly. "Perhaps not. But you meant to create danger, to manufacture spectacle from others' risk. In the end, the difference hardly matters to Captain Mallory."

Brooks sat silent, the last of his practiced charm falling away.

Hartley's voice was quiet but firm. "At Brooklands, we live with danger as a companion, not a commodity. What you did dishonours every driver who faces fear honestly."

Kent gestured to the constables waiting outside. "Lionel Brooks, I am arresting you for the murder of Captain Rex Mallory."

As Brooks was led away, the room seemed to exhale collectively. Ivy studied her gloves, Pym stared unseeing at his papers, and Rae gazed out at the circuit, where the familiar roar of engines was just beginning to rise again.

Bea slipped to Mildred's side. "You did it, Millie. You found the right rhythm in all the noise."

Mildred nodded, feeling not triumph but a tired satisfaction. "It was never about who feared exposure most, it was about who craved attention most desperately. Brooks saw himself not as a killer but as a narrator shaping his own story. That's why he was always just ahead of everyone else, he was writing the script, not merely reporting it."

The library slowly emptied, the drama concluded but its echoes still reverberating. Tomorrow would bring the formal inquest, statements for the papers, and the slow rebuilding of trust. But today, as afternoon light streamed through the windows, Mildred allowed herself to acknowledge that justice, however painful, had finally found its course.

27

The day after Brooks's arrest dawned with that peculiar stillness that often follows upheaval, a quiet made more pronounced by contrast. The usual clamour of engines and banter had given way to hushed conversations; mechanics spoke in lowered voices, committee members moved with an almost performative dignity, and even Mrs Thwaite's kitchen seemed subdued, though the scones remained defiantly light.

Mildred, watching the slow awakening of the circuit from the Clubhouse veranda, felt a curious mixture of satisfaction and melancholy. Justice had been served—Brooks was in custody, his confession recorded in neat police shorthand—yet for Brooklands itself, the ordeal had left scars. Trust was a delicate mechanism; once tampered with, it required more than mere restoration. It needed reimagining.

The mood shifted when she spied Rae St John striding purposefully across the paddock, a sheaf of papers tucked under one arm and her expression set with the stubborn determination Mildred had come to admire. There was something refreshing in Rae's refusal to be dampened by scandal or tragedy; in her brisk, capable movements was the future of Brooklands itself.

By mid-morning, a small but notable crowd had gathered at the pit wall. The racing schedule remained suspended, but the need for community, for some gesture toward continuity, had drawn people from across the club's constituencies. Mildred spotted Hartley, his twin watches properly synchronised; Dr Marsh with her leather valise; a rather subdued Pym standing a little apart; and, somewhat to her surprise, Lady Ivy Carrington, whose orchid corsage seemed almost defiant against her black ensemble.

Rae cleared her throat, and silence fell. "Ladies and gentlemen, this is not a day for speeches. God knows we've had enough talk at Brooklands lately." A murmur of rueful agreement. "But it is a day for looking forward, without forgetting what, and who, we've lost."

She gestured to the curve of the track, gleaming faintly in the thin sunlight. "Captain Mallory believed in making this circuit not just fast, but fair. Not just exciting, but safe. Most of all, he believed knowledge was meant for sharing, not hoarding."

From beside Mildred, Bea whispered, "She's magnificent when she's not being intimidating, isn't she?"

Rae continued, voice steady. "That's why I'm announcing today the establishment of the Mallory Women's Motoring Clinic at Brooklands. A proper school, not just for driving, but for maintenance, safety, and what Mallory called 'poise at speed.' Because women deserve more than decorative roles at the circuit, and men deserve better than to be the only ones risking their necks."

There was a startled pause, then a scattered applause that gained momentum. A few of the older committee members exchanged uncertain glances, but Ivy Carrington, to Mildred's mild surprise, was nodding approvingly.

Mildred stepped forward, sensing the moment's weight. "Miss St John has my full endorsement," she said, her voice carrying clearly. "And my father's foundation will match the first hundred pounds donated to the clinic. Racing is about courage, and courage knows no gender."

The whispers that had begun to ripple at the edges died away. Rae's face showed no gratitude; she was not the sort to need it, but her eyes met Mildred's with a clear, steady respect.

"Applications will be taken starting next week," Rae concluded, her brisk manner returning. "We've space for twenty initially. And yes, there will be buns." She nodded to Mrs Pruett, who beamed with unexpected pride.

As the gathering began to disperse, Mildred noticed Alf Keating lingering at the edge of the pit lane, cap in hand, his weathered face a study in conflicting emotions. Rae approached him directly, extending a slim, oil-smudged envelope.

"This came from Captain Mallory's solicitors this morning," Rae said, her voice pitched for privacy but carrying to where Mildred stood. "It's addressed to you, Mr Keating."

Alf took it with visible trepidation, breaking the seal and scanning the contents. His expression shifted from wariness to disbelief. "It's... it's cleared. The debt. All of it." He looked up, eyes unexpectedly bright. "And there's more. A stipend, for 'maintaining standards in the paddock,' he says."

Rae nodded. "He valued reliability above all else. He knew where to find it."

Alf stared at the letter, his shoulders gradually straightening as if a weight had been physically lifted. "I don't know what to—"

"No need for speeches from you either," Rae cut in, but not unkindly. "But there is a matter I'd like to discuss. The clinic will need a chief mechanic. Someone with patience, experience, and a proper respect for the dangers of cutting corners." She regarded him steadily. "The position is yours, if you want it."

A charged silence followed. Alf's fingers tightened around the paper. "Teaching women to—?"

"To keep themselves alive," Rae finished firmly. "And to understand machines that don't care whether it's a gloved or callused hand at the wheel. Yes or no, Mr Keating?"

He hesitated only a moment longer. "Yes." And then, gruffly, "But I don't go easy on students, man or woman."

"I'd fire you if you did," Rae replied, extending her hand.

Their handshake lingered a moment, Mildred saw it clearly, the way professional respect gave way to something warmer, more uncertain. Two people who had weathered suspicion and scrutiny, finding in each other not romance, perhaps, but a kind of recognition.

Bea, ever observant, murmured, "That's promising. Nothing like mutual competence to spark a flame."

"Let it idle," Mildred replied, smiling. "They'll find their own pace."

The afternoon brought with it a different sort of meeting, one that Mildred herself had arranged with careful thought to both venue and timing. The Clubhouse's private dining room, all polished mahogany and discreet service, would play host to what she had termed a "reform committee." Inspector Kent was there, his notebook conspicuously closed; Hartley sat

THE MYSTERY OF THE FINAL LAP

with perfect posture, both watches laid before him. The unlikely trio of Pym, Lady Ivy, and Dr Marsh completed the circle.

"Thank you all for coming," Mildred began without preamble. "Brooklands has weathered a crisis, but it would be foolish to pretend that Brooks alone was at fault. His crime was enabled by habits and oversights we all participated in."

Pym shifted uncomfortably. "Lady Ramsay, I'm not sure what—"

"Let me be direct, Mr Pym," she interrupted gently. "Your ledgers, while not criminal, reveal a pattern of, shall we say, creative financing. 'Special services' and 'maintenance provisions' that seem to have funded a system of small bribes and inducements."

Kent cleared his throat. "The Yard has reviewed the documents, Mr Pym. There's enough there to merit a formal investigation, unless, of course, full transparency and remediation are forthcoming."

Pym's face had gone grey. "I've done nothing illegal. Merely... expedient."

"Expedience," Mildred replied, "is what allowed Brooks to flourish. He counted on everyone having just enough to hide that no one would look too closely at anyone else."

Hartley tapped the table softly. "What Lady Ramsay proposes, I believe, is a chance to convert personal embarrassment into public benefit."

Pym's gaze darted from face to face, finding no quarter. "What would you have me do?"

"Fund a paddock safety initiative," Mildred said simply. "Openly, transparently, under Yard scrutiny. Make your expertise serve something beyond profit."

For a moment, Pym seemed to consider protest, but the alternative hung unspoken in the air. "Very well," he said at last. "I'll establish a fund. Ten percent of my firm's annual profit, directed to safety infrastructure and training."

"Fifteen," Kent said mildly. "And quarterly reviews of your books."

Pym's jaw tightened, but he nodded. "For how long?"

"Until the initiative is self-sustaining," Mildred replied. "Or until you find you prefer honest reputation to covert influence."

Lady Ivy, who had remained silent throughout this exchange, now straightened in her chair. "And what penance do you have in mind for the committee, Lady Ramsay?" Her tone was light, but her eyes were shrewd. "I doubt our modest financial indiscretions have escaped your notice."

Mildred met her gaze directly. "Your insurance foresight was prudent, Lady Carrington, if cold. But the committee's use of certain 'photographic services' for promotional material borders on exploitation. Mr Sykes's more intimate portraits of drivers and society patrons seem to serve vanity more than sport."

A faint colour touched Ivy's cheeks. "The calendar raises considerable funds."

"Indeed," Mildred agreed. "But at what cost to the dignity of those photographed? Particularly the women drivers, who find their technical achievements secondary to their aesthetic appeal."

Dr Marsh spoke for the first time. "If I may—the clinic Miss St John proposes would benefit greatly from Committee patronage. Not just funding, but the social endorsement only Lady Carrington can provide."

Ivy's expression was unreadable for a moment. Then, with the grace of the truly strategic, she inclined her head. "The Committee would be honoured to redirect its resources toward Miss St John's initiative. The calendar can... evolve its focus to machinery rather than those who operate it."

"And Mr Sykes's services?" Mildred pressed gently.

"Will be retained for technical documentation and proper portraiture," Ivy replied smoothly. "The Committee recognises the changing tide of public taste."

Hartley allowed himself a small, satisfied nod. "I believe Captain Mallory would have approved."

As the meeting adjourned, Mildred found herself standing beside Kent at the window, watching as the first tentative engine tests resumed on the far straight.

"You've engineered quite a reformation," he remarked quietly.

"Only what was already inevitable," she replied. "Brooks showed us the danger of allowing appearances to matter more than substance. Now it's up to Brooklands to remember the lesson."

Outside, Rae was leading a small group—including, Mildred noted with pleasure, three women in practical driving attire—on a tour of the paddock. Alf walked a few paces behind, his expression watchful but no longer haunted.

"Second chances," Mildred murmured, "are rather like engines; they require both careful maintenance and occasional boldness."

Kent smiled. "And a steady hand at the wheel."

As the afternoon light softened over the famous banking, Mildred felt the first real stirrings of resolution. Brooklands would heal, not by forgetting its wounds, but by building something stronger from them. And if the price was a little less glamour and a little more substance, well, that was a bargain worth making.

After all, she thought as Bea joined her with two steaming cups, the best races were always about endurance, not just speed.

28

A fortnight after Brooks's arrest, Brooklands began to shed its shroud of whispers and sidelong glances. The crisp autumn weather had brightened; the last of the season's leaves clung stubbornly to the trees lining the approach road, and a certain purposeful bustle had returned to the paddock. Mechanics no longer worked in tense silence but had reverted to their habitual banter; the press tent, now under new management, clattered with the reassuring sound of legitimate stories being hammered into shape.

Lady Beatrice Mortimer, Bea to her friends, had appointed herself unofficial social architect of this restoration. She stood now at the centre of the Clubhouse lounge, brandishing a clipboard with the exuberance of a field marshal who had finally persuaded her troops to charge in the right direction.

"It was the buns, you know," she announced to the assembled group, which included Mildred, Hartley, Dr Marsh, and a somewhat bemused Constable Blake. "Nothing loosens tongues or tightens community like Mrs Pruett's finest. And now that we've used buns to catch a killer, we must use them to rebuild Brooklands' spirit."

Mildred smiled fondly. "I assume you have a plan beyond pastry?"

"Indeed!" Bea flourished her clipboard. "A ladies' reliability trial to crown the season. Not a race, nothing so vulgar as mere speed, but a demonstration of skill, steadiness, and proper motorcar management. Entry fees to benefit both Captain Mallory's memorial and Rae's clinic."

To Mildred's quiet satisfaction, the idea was met not with scepticism but with immediate, practical engagement. Hartley, as if he'd been anticipating just such a venture, produced a neatly drawn map from his breast pocket.

"A sensible route," he said, smoothing the paper on the table. "Fifty miles encompassing the Surrey lanes, with checkpoints at strategic intervals. Navigation, not just acceleration, will be the test." His moustache twitched with something approaching enthusiasm. "I've taken the liberty of marking ideal refuelling points."

Dr Marsh nodded approvingly. "I'll arrange first aid stations. Nothing dramatic expected, but preparation is prudent. And I suspect we might get a few of the nursing volunteers from the war effort to assist, many haven't lost their taste for motors and medicine."

Constable Blake, his official reserve momentarily abandoned, stepped forward with the eagerness of a schoolboy. "I'd be honoured to wave the starter's flag, Lady Mortimer, if that would be appropriate?" He reddened slightly at his own enthusiasm.

"Entirely appropriate," Bea assured him. "We need a representative of law and order to remind everyone that reliability includes obeying the Highway Code."

Mrs Pruett, who had been hovering at the edge of the gathering, could contain herself no longer. "And I'll provide currant buns at every checkpoint! For truth's sake, and because no one thinks straight on an empty stomach."

The laughter that followed had a healing quality to it; genuine, unforced, the sound of a community remembering how to be more than a collection of suspicions. As the group expanded to include Alf, several committee secretaries, and even Lady Ivy (who graciously offered the orchid room for planning meetings), Mildred felt the atmosphere transform. The talk became a blend of logistics and light-hearted debate: whether Yorkshire drivers might be allowed to compete despite their "excessive northern caution" (Bea's term), what constituted a reasonable time penalty for an improperly stowed picnic basket, and whether gentlemen might serve as navigators without "undue interference with the ladies' concentration."

Later, as the golden late afternoon stretched shadows across the circuit, Mildred found herself walking the Finishing Straight with Inspector Kent. The gravel crunched pleasantly beneath their feet; the banking curved away in its magnificent arc, somehow more dignified for having witnessed both tragedy and justice.

"You seem satisfied," Kent observed, his stride matching hers.

"With the outcome, yes," Mildred replied. "Though satisfaction feels too simple a word for justice served."

"Indeed." Kent paused, gazing out at the empty track. "There are still loose ends to tidy, of course. Sykes has been dismissed, though not without a severance that suggests Lady Carrington prefers his silence to his services. Pym's accounts have been surrendered to my colleagues at the financial branch; they'll keep him honest, if not entirely comfortable."

"And Rae's clinic?"

Kent's expression warmed. "The schedule is posted in the paddock. Twenty-six applicants already, including two rather distinguished dowagers who claim they're tired of relying on chauffeurs with 'artistic temperaments.'"

Mildred laughed. "They'll find Rae has quite enough temperament of her own. But a steadier hand on the tiller, I think."

They walked on in companionable silence for a moment.

"I'll be required back in London soon," Kent said at last. "The paperwork alone will keep a desk sergeant busy for a week. But I may return for Lady Mortimer's reliability trial."

"Oh?"

His eyes crinkled at the corners. "If the buns return, so shall I. One develops a taste for both justice and currants in this profession."

From behind them came the sound of approaching footsteps, Bea, resplendent in a new motoring scarf, clipboard still at the ready.

"Inspector! I've just added you to the judges' panel, if you've no objection. We need someone with an eye for detail and an appreciation for the finer points of rule-following."

Kent bowed slightly. "I would be honoured, Lady Mortimer."

Bea executed a playful curtsy. "Excellent! Mildred, darling, I've put you down for the opening address. Something about tradition and innovation, you always strike the right note."

She hurried off, already calling to Alf about tool-check demonstrations and the proper scoring for "bonnets closed with style."

"She is indomitable," Kent remarked.

"Thank goodness," Mildred replied. "Without Bea's particular blend of frivolity and purpose, I fear we'd all be rather too solemn for comfort."

As the day's light began to soften toward evening, Mildred found herself reluctant to leave. The modest motorcar she had driven during her dawn lesson with Rae, the very vehicle that had demonstrated the saboteur's routes and methods, had been discreetly made available to her. Rae had insisted, in her typically direct fashion, that "someone with sense ought to have it, and you're the only one who didn't flinch at forty on the banking."

Now, as the circuit quieted and the mechanics began to pack away their tools, Mildred stood on the Clubhouse steps with Kent beside her. The fading light cast everything in gentle blue shadow, softening the harsh lines of recent memory.

"Will you come again to Brooklands, Inspector?" she asked. "Beyond the reliability trial, I mean."

Kent considered the question with his characteristic thoroughness. "I believe I shall. There are qualities here worth preserving, courage, certainly, but also a particular kind of honesty that emerges when speed meets skill."

"And occasional nonsense," Mildred added.

"That too." He smiled; a genuine expression, not the professional mask he had worn so often during the investigation. "In my line of work, Lady Ramsay, one sees too many places broken beyond repair. It would be a privilege to witness this one heal."

Their eyes met, and something passed between them, not quite a promise, certainly not a goodbye, but a recognition of shared purpose that transcended the immediate case. Justice had been their common ground; compassion, perhaps, would be their continuing path.

The moment was broken by the distant sound of an engine being tested, a clean, eager note that spoke of mechanical health rather than threat. Kent checked his watch.

"Tomorrow's testing begins at nine," he said. "Order restored, even to the timetable."

"Reputations mended," Mildred added, "futures quietly set in motion."

Across the circuit, the last mechanics were leaving, tool bags slung over their shoulders. Alf lingered at the garage door, ostensibly checking a last lock but clearly waiting as Rae completed her notes at a makeshift desk. Their silhouettes, outlined against the paddock lights, spoke of comfortable companionship, colleagues, perhaps more, but certainly equals in their devotion to craft.

Bea emerged from the Clubhouse, coat draped over her arm. "Ready, Mildred? The car's waiting, and Mrs Thwaite has promised a proper dinner. She says we deserve it, after 'all that detecting business.'"

Kent tipped his hat to them both. "Ladies. Until the reliability trial."

As they parted ways, Kent to his temporary lodgings, Mildred and Bea to the waiting motorcar, Mildred took a last look at Brooklands in the gathering twilight. Its curves and straights, its banks and pits, its clubhouse and paddock—all places where ambition met skill, where courage faced fear, and where, despite the occasional darkness, light and speed would always find their way forward.

In the distance, engines ticked cool, their day's work done. Tomorrow's run would begin at nine as it should, as it must.

For all the scandal and suspicion, Brooklands endured. And in its endurance was a lesson Mildred would carry with her: that communities, like the best racing machines, require both careful maintenance and the occasional courage to rebuild what has broken.

She slipped behind the wheel of her modest car, feeling the satisfying grip of the controls beneath her gloved hands. Bea settled beside her with a contented sigh.

"Home, then?" Bea asked.

"Home," Mildred agreed, starting the engine with newfound confidence. "But perhaps we'll take the scenic route. I find I'm rather developing a taste for the open road."

And as they drove away, leaving Brooklands to its evening peace, Mildred knew that while this particular mystery was solved, the greater adventure—of justice tempered with mercy, of truth balanced with kindness—would continue. Just as the circuit would welcome new drivers, new races, new triumphs and occasional heartbreaks, so too would she find new puzzles, new communities in need.

But for now, there was the purr of a well-tuned engine, the companionship of a dear friend, and the quiet satisfaction of knowing that, in at least this corner of Surrey, all was right with the world.

The End

AFTERWORD

Thank you for reading **The Mystery of the Final Lap**. I really hope you enjoyed reading it as much as I had writing it!

If you have a minute, please consider leaving a review on Amazon or the retailer where you got it.

Many thanks in advance for your support!

THE MYSTERY OF THE VANISHING VIOLINIST

CHAPTER 1 SNEAK PEEK

The last rays of a mild spring evening filtered through the vast glass dome of the Royal Albert Hall, bathing the gathering crowd in a soft golden glow that made even the most modest evening attire shimmer with elegant promise. Lady Mildred Ramsay paused in the entrance foyer, her dark eyes taking in the scene with quiet appreciation. After the wind-swept grittiness of the Brooklands racing circuit during their last adventure and the quiet seclusion of Highfield Manor before that, the grandeur of London's premier concert venue was a welcome change of scenery.

"Do hurry along, Millie," her brother Henry called from several paces ahead, consulting his pocket watch with a furrowed brow. "We're cutting it terribly fine. The Duke of Hathersfield has reserved seats in his private box, and it simply wouldn't do to arrive after the first movement."

"Heaven forbid we should inconvenience His Grace by being fashionably late," Mildred replied with gentle mockery, though she quickened her pace to appease her brother's sense of propriety. Henry had always been the embodiment of punctuality and protocol, his military bearing testament to years of service. Even now, two years after the Armistice, he carried himself with ramrod straightness, his sandy brown hair neatly parted, his evening attire impeccable.

"It's not merely a matter of inconvenience," Henry insisted, guiding them through the elegant throng towards the grand staircase. "This is a charity concert for war widows and orphans. The Duke chairs the committee, and considering our family's connection to the cause—"

"I'm well aware of the significance, Henry," Mildred cut in, more gently now. Her years as a VAD nurse during the Great War had left her with a profound understanding of such causes. "I merely suggested that arriving three minutes before the programme begins hardly constitutes tardiness."

At that moment, Lady Beatrice Mortimer caught up to them in a whirl of pale blue silk and golden curls, her diminutive figure darting between bemused concert-goers with the agility of a sparrow.

"There you are!" she exclaimed, linking her arm through Mildred's. "I was beginning to think you'd abandoned me to the tender mercies of Lady Carrington, who's wearing the most absurd turban with feathers that nearly took out poor Mr Sykes's eye when she turned too quickly." She lowered her voice to a theatrical whisper. "And speaking of eyes, have you seen Captain Wilcox in his evening dress? The man looks positively edible."

"Bea," Henry admonished, though his lips twitched with reluctant amusement. "We're at a charitable function, not a matchmaking salon."

"Darling Henry, one can appreciate beauty while supporting a worthy cause," Bea replied with a wink. "Besides, the Captain has made a tremendous donation. Rumour has it he's pursuing a knighthood."

THE MYSTERY OF THE VANISHING VIOLINIST

As they ascended the grand staircase, Mildred observed the vibrant tableau of London society in full evening regalia. Ladies in fashionable dropped-waist gowns with glittering beadwork and feathered headbands moved in graceful counterpoint to gentlemen in immaculate black tie. The air thrummed with excited chatter and the lingering scent of expensive perfume.

"The Dowager Countess of Milford has come out of mourning at last," Bea continued, nodding discreetly towards an elderly woman in lavender silk. "Though if you ask me, it's less about the appropriate passage of time and more about Anton Lanyi's performance. They say she hasn't missed one of his concerts since he arrived from Budapest."

"The Hungarian virtuoso has certainly caused quite a stir," Henry remarked as they reached the first-floor landing. "The programme was sold out within hours of being announced."

Mildred nodded, recalling what she had read about the celebrated violinist. Anton Lanyi had emerged from the chaos of post-war Central Europe as a musical sensation, his passionate interpretations of both classical works and his own compositions earning him rapturous reviews across the Continent. His arrival in London had been heralded as the cultural event of the season.

"They say his Stradivarius was smuggled out of Hungary during the worst of the troubles," Bea whispered, eyes alight with intrigue. "Wrapped in oilcloth and hidden in a false compartment of a refugee's cart. Can you imagine?"

"I imagine much of what one hears about Maestro Lanyi is carefully cultivated to enhance his mystique," Mildred replied pragmatically. "Though I don't doubt the upheaval in his homeland has shaped his art."

They paused at the entrance to the Duke's private box, where a uniformed attendant checked their invitation cards with stiff formality. As they were ushered inside, Mildred's gaze was drawn to the magnificent auditorium below. Tier upon tier of crimson and gold circled the central space, where the orchestra had begun to assemble on the stage. The enormous pipe organ loomed majestically at the far end, its polished pipes gleaming in the electric light that had recently replaced the original gas illumination.

"How perfectly splendid," Bea murmured, settling into her plush seat. "I do adore the Royal Albert Hall. It's simply the most romantic venue in London."

"I suspect the Prince Consort had more elevated notions than romance when he envisioned it," Henry remarked dryly, arranging the programme notes on his lap with military precision.

"Oh, pish," Bea dismissed with a wave. "Albert was desperately romantic. Why else build such a gloriously extravagant monument to the arts? Besides, just look around—half the affairs in London society begin in these boxes during the interval." She leaned closer to Mildred, nodding towards an adjacent box. "Speaking of which, is that not Mrs Harrington with Colonel Foster? I was quite certain she was meant to be in Bath visiting her ailing mother."

"Bea, really," Mildred admonished, though she couldn't help but follow her friend's gaze. "You've become positively Machiavellian in your interest in other people's indiscretions."

"Not Machiavellian, darling—merely observant. A quality you've taught me to cultivate, I might add." Bea's blue eyes twinkled mischievously. "Though I do wonder what Lady Harrington would say if she knew her husband was escorting the Colonel's wife while she's supposedly nursing her mother through a bout of pleurisy that seems remarkably convenient."

Henry cleared his throat pointedly. "If you two have quite finished dissecting the moral failings of our social circle, the concert is about to begin."

Indeed, the house lights had begun to dim, and a hush fell over the packed auditorium. Mildred settled back in her seat, allowing the atmosphere to wash over her. Despite Bea's frivolity and Henry's stuffiness, she was genuinely looking forward to the evening's performance. Music had always been a refuge for her, especially after the chaos and suffering she had witnessed during the war. There was something about the mathematical precision of classical compositions that soothed her analytical mind while still allowing space for emotion.

As the conductor took his place on the podium to polite applause, Mildred found herself scanning the crowd below. It was a habit she had developed during her nursing days and refined during her unexpected forays into criminal investigation—this quiet observation of human behaviour from a slight remove. She noted Lady Ivy Carrington's strategic positioning near the royal box, the tension in Mrs Sylvia Harcourt's shoulders as she whispered urgently to her companion, the studied boredom of Lord Ravenshaw despite his obvious interest in the young violinist seated in the orchestra's first chair.

The typical games of society, Mildred thought with a small smile. So predictable and yet so endlessly fascinating in their subtle variations. She had never been one for active participation in such theatrics, preferring the role of observer to that of performer. Her natural reticence, combined with her keen eye for detail and logical mind, had served her well both as a nurse and, more recently, as an amateur detective.

The conductor raised his baton, and the first notes of Mozart filled the cavernous space. Bea sighed contentedly, Henry relaxed incrementally, and Mildred allowed herself to be momentarily transported, all thoughts of society intrigue temporarily set aside.

For now, she was simply a woman enjoying beautiful music in a magnificent setting, flanked by her occasionally exasperating but ultimately beloved brother and friend. Tomorrow might bring new puzzles, new challenges, even new dangers—but tonight was for Mozart, for charity, and for the simple pleasure of being alive in a world that, despite its many flaws, still contained such transcendent beauty.

As the music swelled around them, Mildred couldn't know that within hours, this peaceful moment would be shattered. That the celebrated violinist, who was yet to make his appearance, would soon be at the centre of a mystery that would test her skills and resolve in ways she could not imagine. For now, she simply listened, her dark eyes reflective, her sharp mind temporarily at rest, unaware that fate had once again placed her in the vicinity of impending tragedy.

Get your copy at all good retailers.

ALSO BY RUTH BAKER

The Ivy Creek Cozy Mystery Series

Which Pie Goes with Murder? (Book 1)

Twinkle, Twinkle, Deadly Sprinkles (Book 2)

Eat Once, Die Twice (Book 3)

Silent Night, Unholy Bites (Book 4)

Waffles and Scuffles (Book 5)

Cookie Dough and Bruised Egos (Book 6)

A Sticky Toffee Catastrophe (Book 7)

Dough Shall Not Murder (Book 8)

Deadly Bites on Winter Nights (Book 9)

A Juicy Steak Tragedy (Book 10)

Southern Fried and Grief Stricken (Book 11)

Poisoned Freebies at Phoebe's (Book 12)

Tasty Edibles, Nasty Rumblings (Book 13)

A Spicy Side of Homicide (Book 14)

The Wedding Cake Conundrum (Book 15)

The Whispering Haven Cozy Mystery Series

Gone in a Snap (Book 1)

Say Cheese and Die Laughing (Book 2)

Deadly Flash from the Past (Book 3)

Framed in Mischief (Book 4)

Silent Night, Deadly Light (Book 5)

Focal Point Fiasco (Book 6)

The Lady Mildred Ramsay Murder Mystery Series

The Mystery of the Disappearing Diamonds (Book 1)
The Mystery of the Final Lap (Book 2)
The Mystery of the Vanishing Violinist (Book 3)

NEWSLETTER SIGNUP

Want **FREE** COPIES OF FUTURE **CLEANTALES** BOOKS, FIRST NOTIFICATION OF NEW RELEASES, CONTESTS AND GIVEAWAYS?

GO TO THE LINK BELOW TO SIGN UP TO THE NEWSLETTER!

https://cleantales.com/newsletter/

Printed in Dunstable, United Kingdom